Angelique didn't seem to have anything at all to say as they strode beneath the deep blue sky toward the palace.

Valentine took her through the back entrance to his quarters, up three flights of steps carved into stone and circling around and around until they reached a door that led directly into his bedroom via a hidden passageway and wall panel.

She stepped through and looked around, then gazed back toward the tunnel that led to the stairs. "Handy," she murmured.

"Shall I send for refreshments?"

"I'm probably not staying."

"Any particular reason why?"

She nodded, took a deep breath. "I'm pregnant."

"Excuse me?"

"Pregnant."

He had no words.

"To you," she added and lifted her chin.

"That's impossible."

"Well, clearly it's not!"

Claimed by a King

Irresistible royal passion!

Meet the powerful rulers of Byzenmaach, Liesendaach, Arun and Thallasia.

Their royal duty must come before everything.

Nothing and *no one* can distract them.

But how can Casimir, Theodosius, Augustus and Valentine deny the fierce flames of desire when they meet the only women ever to threaten their iron resolve?

Read Casimir of Byzenmaach's story in
Shock Heir for the Crown Prince

Read Theodosius of Liesendaach's story in
Convenient Bride for the King

Read Augustus of Arun's story in
Untouched Queen by Royal Command

And Valentine of Thallasia's story in
Pregnant in the King's Palace

Don't miss this sinful, sexy quartet by Kelly Hunter!

Kelly Hunter

PREGNANT IN THE KING'S PALACE

HARLEQUIN
PRESENTS

ISBN-13: 978-1-335-40415-2

Pregnant in the King's Palace

This edition published by arrangement with Harlequin Books S.A.

For questions and comments about the quality of this book,
please contact us at CustomerService@Harlequin.com.

Harlequin Enterprises ULC
22 Adelaide St. West, 40th Floor
Toronto, Ontario M5H 4E3, Canada
www.Harlequin.com

Printed in U.S.A.

Recycling programs
for this product may
not exist in your area.

Kelly Hunter has always had a weakness for fairy tales, fantasy worlds and losing herself in a good book. She has two children, avoids cooking and cleaning and, despite the best efforts of her family, is no sports fan. Kelly is, however, a keen gardener and has a fondness for roses. Kelly was born in Australia and has traveled extensively. Although she enjoys living and working in different parts of the world, she still calls Australia home.

Visit the Author Profile page
at Harlequin.com for more titles.

PROLOGUE

'YOU'RE NOT FOOLING ANYONE, you know.'

Prince Valentine of Thallasia was eighteen years old, heir to an age-old kingdom and accountable to very few. His father ruled supreme and expected instant obedience and got it. His mother was long dead. His twin sister was the only other person he listened to, on occasion, and she'd definitely upped her scolding of late. Granted, her scolding often served to burst his bubble of entitlement and superiority—and theoretically this was a good thing. Kept him grounded or modest or some such. But he didn't have to like it.

His sister matched him stride for stride as they headed across manicured lawns towards the sprawling stone stable complex. The royal palace employed over a dozen stable hands alongside a dedicated stable master. They currently had over six strings of polo ponies in training at the palace, not to mention a dozen or so racehorses. Their father was a horse-riding fanatic and, until recently, Valentine had remained happily free of that particular bug. 'I have no idea what you're talking about.'

'This sudden interest you have in horses and riding them every chance you get.'

'What can I say? It's spring. I want to be outdoors.'

'It's spring and you want into the new stable girl's pants,' Vala replied dryly. 'Everyone sees it, everyone knows it. You have the subtlety of a stallion around a mare in heat. Not that you've ever seen a stallion around a mare in heat because until recently your interest in our royal horseflesh has been nonexistent.'

'And now I'm rectifying that lack.' He smirked because he knew it would irritate her. 'You should be praising me.'

'I'm trying to warn you, you dolt. Father's not going to approve of your choice of plaything.'

'She has a name.'

'And that's exactly the attitude that's going to get you into more trouble than either you or Angelique Cordova can deal with. Yes, I know her name. Don't look so surprised. I like her, she's smart and outspoken and far too beautiful for anyone's good, and if you take things further with her and Father finds out he'll break her and he'll do it in front of you.'

'Just because he hasn't found anyone to replace our mother—'

'Oh, don't even go there!' His sister had a temper and she wasn't shy about showing it. 'Father lost interest in our dear departed mother as soon as he bred her and got us. He goes through mistresses faster than most people go through tissues and there are never any complications. No fuss, no noise, no royal bastards. Ever. Do you want to know what happens to those women foolish enough to try and trap him? Because I hear rumours and they are ugly and I believe them.'

They were almost at the stables, a centuries-old stone building buttressing the palace walls. The palace had been built to withstand sieges, way back when, and although the walls had come down to the east to make way for a grand entry road and gardens, far grimmer sections of the building existed, tucked in behind the beautiful façade. One of the reasons he hadn't liked coming to the stables before now was that he could feel the weight of oppression and ugliness bearing down on him there—no matter how beautiful and expensive the horses. Not that he had any intention of telling his sister he was afraid of ghosts.

Or that, no matter how much he didn't want to believe her savage assessment of his father, she might be right.

He wanted this conversation to be over so he could get on with the business of admiring Angelique, but his twin put her hand to his forearm and forced him to turn and stop. 'Valentine, whatever's wrong with Father, it's getting worse. The rages. The cruelty. And even you: Crown Prince, heir apparent, God's anointed…you're not immune any more, the way you were as a child when you thought he walked on water and wanted to be just like him. He sees you as competition now and nothing good is going to come of it. He will envy you, pull rank on you, and crush her. I can see it coming, plain as day, even if you can't.'

He didn't want to hear it. 'Look, I know he can be hard to please. He's not…good…with women. With you. I see that.'

His sister laughed, bright and bitter. 'I am the prettiest dress-up doll in the room, and as long as I stay that way, he will adore me. I aim to marry early and get gone from here just as soon as I can. Better still if I can make it seem like his idea.' She held his gaze, her dark eyes imploring. 'But you… you need to be careful who you take up with, okay? And how you go about it. Don't play with your pretty toys in front of him. Don't ever let your infatuation with Angelique turn into something else. Above all, practise safe sex.'

'Seriously? You're giving me the sex talk?'

'I'm giving you a *warning*. Bad things happen to women who get pregnant by father. Bad things happen to women who defy him in other ways. Ask around if you don't believe me.'

'You have *no* idea what you're talking about.' His sister always had been melodramatic, full of plots and palace intrigues, but of all the undesirable things he *had* heard, he'd never heard *that*. Their father had his faults, but he wasn't a monster.

'I am dead serious about this, Valentine.' Her eyes flashed cold fire. 'Why do you always think you know better than anyone else? Why can't you just *listen* to what I'm telling you?'

He was. He did. She'd never knowingly steered him wrong. 'All right,' he grated. 'I'll be discreet.'

'See that you are.'

Valentine brooded on his sister's opinion of their father as she stormed off towards the new brood mares. Yes, their father was a distant figure, not given to praise. Discipline was harsh—his father had no use for weaklings because ruling a kingdom took strength. As for his father's way with women… Valentine didn't see malice in it. Indifference, yes. High turnover, yes. Wasn't as if he were cruel in his dismissal of them. They came, they went. No fanfare, no problem. His father had needs, that was all. And Valentine was his father's son.

Surely his father would know that Valentine had no intention of going to his wedding bed a virgin? And that he had no intention of marrying *anyone* any time soon, let alone the pretty stable girl? Even Angelique knew that whatever interest he showed in her, an offer of marriage wouldn't be part of it.

She wasn't a permanent employee, she'd be gone within the year, which to his way of thinking would be just about perfect. Angelique had arrived with six of her family's stunning Cordova mares, hand-picked by his father and hers to temporarily become part of the palace's breeding programme. One year, one drop of foals, less than seven months remaining and then the foals would be on the ground and the mares would be gone and Angelique with them.

It wasn't a *bad* thing, his infatuation. More like the perfect opportunity to live a little, love a little, and learn how to please a woman. Because, heaven help him, he dreamed about pleasing Angelique. He dreamed about possessing her so completely she'd never forget him and more often than not he woke in a lather of sweat and spent desire, no matter how often he took himself in hand. How was that *healthy*? If he could just *have* her for a time… get her out of his system…all would be well, and he could get on with the business of finding a suitable queen for Thallasia.

His sister was wrong about their father's viciousness and instability. His father would understand.

Valentine of Thallasia was eighteen years old, firstborn son of a king, and used to claiming whatever he wanted.

And he wanted Angelique.

Valentine strode through the main corridor of the stable complex as if he owned it. Which, technically, he one day would. Stable master Alessandro nodded in acknowledgement. Nothing happened in these stables without that man's notice and that was both a good and bad thing.

His sister's words reverberated in his brain like a persistent little hammer. It probably *wouldn't* hurt to avoid Angelique for the time being and pretend actual interest in the horse-breeding programme and see if he could be of any real assistance. He wasn't against learning about the horse-breeding programmes of kings. As for riding, he could always improve. There were lessons to be learned here. Strengths to be gained. At least be discreet—*that* was his sister's take-home message. *That* he could do.

An hour and a half later, Valentine left Alessandro's office, his brain full of bloodlines and horse names and a new appreciation for the mares on loan to Thallasia. The Cordova name was an old one in horse-breeding circles. A fully trained Cordova horse had been a gift fit for a king for the last three centuries and more. Money and power, passion and status, and Angelique was no mere stable girl—she was royalty of a different kind and all the more irresistible because of it.

Finally, he allowed himself to seek her out. Only natural for him to want to approach the source, given the information he'd just inhaled. And there she stood, hosing sweat from the flank of a just-exercised horse—her pale jodhpurs, knee-high black boots and cotton T-shirt wreaking havoc on what little restraint he claimed to have. His father's second-best stallion was currently behaving like a day-old lamb beneath her hands, but that didn't stop him from offering his assistance. Not that she took it. Instead she rolled her eyes and tucked a stray strand of hair behind one ear. Silky black and falling to her waist, her hair fell in waves like the sea, and she plaited it when working—a single thick rope that fell between her shoulder blades and continued to her hips—but he'd seen it undone once, and he would see it like that again if he had his way. Bury his fists in it the better to tilt her face towards his and—

'You keep looking at me like that and I'm going to hose *you* down,' she told him, and it didn't sound like a threat. More like a promise.

'You wouldn't dare.' He summoned his most engaging grin. 'Because if you *did* I'd have to take my wet shirt off in front of you.' Which as far as he was concerned was win-win.

She laughed and reached for the plastic scraper and began applying it to the horse's back. 'I've seen better bodies.'

Doubtful.

She spared him a glance and laughed. 'You are the smuggest boy I've ever met.'

'Man. Smuggest *man* you've ever met,' he corrected, and she laughed again and it was a beautiful sound.

'Angelique,' Alessandro barked from inside a nearby stall. 'Get on with it.'

'See? You've got me into trouble. Some of us are working.' But she didn't sound concerned. Maybe because she was in the unique position of being beholden to her family's horses first and the royal stables of Thallasia second. It gave her a boldness the other grooms didn't have, not to mention that she was the best rider amongst them by far, with an uncanny instinct for getting the best out of any horse beneath her. He knew for a fact that Alessandro used her shamelessly to help train the more advanced horses here.

'How many horses do you still have to exercise?'

'Your father's best stallion and my favourite Cordova mare.'

The two most impressive beasts in the complex. He'd learned that of late, and naturally he wanted to master both of them. 'Want some help there?'

She straightened slowly, taking her sweet time looking him over. She wasn't indifferent to him, far from it, and this game they played was delicious. 'Are you up to it?'

Surely he could be forgiven for groaning his reply. 'Alessandro, I'm taking my father's stallion up to the gamekeeper's lodge. Will that count as his exercise for the day?'

The older man's head and shoulders appeared above a stall wall. 'Do you have your father's permission?'

'Well, he didn't say no.' Possibly because Valentine hadn't yet asked him. 'Can Angelique come with me?'

The horsemaster spared her a hard glance and a

string of rapid Spanish. Angelique nodded and replied in kind.

'Was that a yes?' he asked.

'That was a don't encourage you and definitely
don't get you killed. There was also a be careful in
there and an I hope you know what you're doing.'

'So it *was* a yes.'

'Only if you're the one riding the mare.'

'*Excuse me?*'

'That stallion's crawling out of his skin today on
account of servicing a mare yesterday. We sent the
mare to pasture at one of your farms this morning
and I swear he can still smell her. If we ride, I'm
the one who'll be riding him because he's an ill-
mannered pig. *You* will have the pleasure of riding
a perfectly trained Cordova mare.'

'See, that's what I thought you said the first time.
I just can't comprehend the "you riding the stallion
instead of me" part.'

She gave a gallic little shrug and pointed towards
the stallion's stall. 'Me, that one.' She pointed towards a different stall. 'You, that one. She's faster
than the big brute anyway.'

'Want to bet?' It was the only way he could tolerate the assault on his masculinity.

'I love to bet.'

It took twenty more minutes before they were riding out towards the heavily forested western edges
of the palace grounds. Another thirty before they
reached the gamekeeper's lodge. He was the first

to dismount. He tried not to stare as she slid lightly from the horse and stared at the lodge with her hands on her hips and her head tilted to one side.

'Would you like to go in?' he asked.

'Are there any other people in there?'

'No.'

'Then, no. If you want to bed me—and you do— you might try getting to know me first.'

'I already know a lot about you.' Nothing but the truth. She came from a centuries-old Spanish horse-breeding and training family with extensive holdings in the Pyrenees. Her mother was from Liesendaach originally—the kingdom adjoining his—but had embraced her new country with a wide-open heart. Angelique had an identical twin sister and an older brother. She liked to rise before dawn and take a two-hour lunch at midday and then work again until late. She feared no horse or man—which in his opinion was a mistake. She was beyond beautiful and he wasn't the only one who'd noticed. In his more cynical moments he'd almost convinced himself he'd be doing her a favour by making his interest in her so plain. Some of his father's men had hungry eyes and brutal ways and they were looking, no mistake.

His sister's warning hammered away at his conscience, and something…he didn't know what… made him say, 'You should go home soon. Don't stay.' He had no idea where his chivalrous streak was coming from. 'Let Alessandro look to the welfare of your father's mares. Come back at foaling time. Better still, don't come back here at all.'

'Why?' He had her attention, every last scrap of it. He wanted to preen and puff and show off beneath that breathtaking face and steady gaze.

'It's not safe for you here. You're too—'

She waited, but he didn't know how to phrase what he wanted to say. 'Too what?'

Too wild, too innocent, too beautiful to resist. Too much. 'Too tempting for this court of crows,' he settled for saying instead. 'You've drawn attention and not just mine. Your father should know better than to send you here. He should have sent his son.'

She dropped her gaze to the ground and toed the edge of the manicured grass with her boot. 'And what if my brother would have been even more vulnerable than me?'

'He wouldn't be.'

Such a strange little smile as she stared at him from beneath that stray chunk of hair and he wanted nothing more than to reach out and touch it, push it gently from her face. Slowly, he reached out to do just that.

She didn't pull away.

'You don't know anything about my brother or me. I can take care of myself.' And if her voice trembled almost as much as his fingers had, neither of them made mention of it.

'What's your favourite food?' he asked.

'Mangoes and strawberries.'

'Your favourite drink?'

'Good café solo. Of which you have none!'

He could fix that. 'And where do you like to be kissed?'

Because he'd make that move next. His insides clenched with the promise of it, and the air between them grew syrupy with waiting.

'Here,' she murmured at last, touching her fingers to a place on her neck.

'Got it.' He logged the spot with his fingers, heat pooling low in his body and causing a stir as she arched her neck as if inviting more. She was warm beneath his fingertips, her skin soft to the touch, and her hair held the scent of summer. He could feel her racing pulse—or maybe it was his. 'Where else?'

She slid her fingers towards the place where jaw met ear. 'Here.'

He set his lips to the first place and slowly dragged his way to the next and she trembled for him and made a faint whimper that sounded like encouragement. 'Yes?' He barely recognised his own voice, the rough, needy edge of it.

She turned her head, her lips found his and that was all the answer he needed. He didn't stop until he was sated and neither did she. From the shadow of the lodge to its entrance hall and then the trophy room with its massive leather sofa that they put to wicked use.

Over and over again, in the weeks that followed.

With every sly challenge and laughing touch she

dug beneath his skin until he could barely think of anything but when next he could have her. Never mind his father's men, who watched them with increasing suspicion. Never mind his sister, who covered for his absence on more than one occasion and told him over and over to be careful and discreet and *for God's sake, Valentine, grow some survival skills*.

He was the firstborn son of a king. He couldn't afford to love as he would. He *knew* this.

Angelique knew it too. They'd talked about what he could offer her and it wasn't much. She was the wrong nationality and moreover she worked for a living. Her education was sorely lacking. He would one day marry a well-bred daughter of Thallasia— bonus points if she had political ties the monarchy could use to advantage. Such was the family firm he'd been born to. They *knew* this. Accepted it. They weren't playing for keeps.

They were just playing.

Her favourite city was Salamanca. Her favourite meal was her mother's paella marinera. There was nothing in this world he craved more than the time they spent together, learning how to please her. Her uninhibited cries as he devoured her. The clench and release of her pleasure.

He knew he was neglecting his regular duties. This reckless abandon had to stop before he handed Angelique Cordova the keys to his heart and soul in addition to the ones to his body.

But he didn't say this had to end as Angelique

rolled out of his embrace and started putting on her clothes, chiding him to do the same because they had to get back because she'd be missed if they were late. As it was, they'd have to hurry back, and Alessandro the stable master would know it due to the lather of the horses.

'Race you,' he challenged, and she took him at his word. Always the unruly stallion for her and the well-behaved mare for him. Alessandro could overlook many things but risking the Crown Prince's neck on an unreliable horse was not one of them.

Race you and you're on, with the scent of her drying on his skin.

His father was waiting for them.

CHAPTER ONE

KING VALENTINE OF THALLASIA was a wanted man.
His royal blood, his country's wealth and his striking
looks made sure of that. He'd been angelically pretty
as a child and an unrepentantly precocious teen.
There'd been a time in his twenties when his reckless reputation had kept all but the most experienced
women at bay. At twenty-eight he'd become engaged
to a perfectly presentable, blue-blooded heiress with
many fine qualities. He'd been pressured to appear
steady and ready to ascend the throne in the face of
his father's failing health, she'd been present, and
he'd liked her well enough. She'd ticked all the boxes
his palace courtiers had wanted her to tick. Well
bred, well educated, well versed when it came to
mixing with the high-born and observing royal protocol. Above all, she'd made him look good.

He'd broken their three-year engagement last
night, and the pity had rolled off her in waves as
she'd handed back his mother's ring, kissed his
cheek and told him to take care. His former beloved

had asked that he wait a day before announcing their split in order to give her time to return to her father's private estate. She didn't want to deal with the media and their questions, she'd said. Given the delicacy of the information he might or might not want to reveal, she much preferred to leave the details to him.

He'd yet to decide if her actions had been cowardly or merciful.

Either way she was gone, and the charity polo weekend in the kingdom of Liesendaach was in full swing. He could have gone home this morning, citing some fictitious royal crisis or other, and his host and childhood friend, King Theodosius, would have understood. Instead, he'd chosen to stay on alone, and Theo, as if sensing a ripple in the ether, was sticking close.

They'd managed to find a relatively private spot to watch the current polo match—a cue for a private conversation. Theo had doubtless engineered the moment and Valentine wondered with dark amusement just how long Theo would hold back his questions. Perhaps a pre-empt was in order. It was that or compliment the man on his beautiful gardens and immaculately kept playing fields, and Theo had probably heard that a dozen times already this morning. Of all the four kingdoms in the land, Theo's palace was the prettiest. The fussiest, King Casimir of Byzenmaach often called it with a sly grin. Pretentious, King Augustus of Arun would murmur, joining in. Fact was, their palaces were grey, gloomy and austere in comparison. And for all the improvements he'd made to *his* palace lately, it was still no match for Theo's. 'I'm no longer betrothed.'

Theo didn't so much as blink. 'I figured as much when your former intended made her apologies this morning and left before breakfast, her fingers bare. My condolences. I liked her well enough.'

'Faint praise.'

'I never thought *you* liked her well enough.' Theo shrugged and turned to watch the play. 'So what's next?'

Good question. Great question. But further confession seemed to stick in his throat and stay there.

Silence fell between them after that. The assessing looks his childhood friend kept shooting him made the imaginary bullseye between his shoulders twitch. 'Out with it,' he demanded after one twitch too many. 'I know that look. You're plotting.'

'Not plotting,' Theo denied smoothly. 'Just thinking.'

'About *what*?'

'Do you realise that you and Angelique Cordova never get within a hundred feet of each other? Is that choreographed? Do you practise?'

'I have no idea what you're talking about.' Valentine knew exactly what Theo was talking about, he simply wasn't about to admit it. 'Although I do note, with casual interest, just how close you've become to the Cordova family of late.'

'Moriana has taken Angelique and her sister Luciana under her wing.'

'Is that wise?' Valentine had never quite forgiven Theo for dallying with both Angelique and Luciana Cordova a few years back. Rumour had it they'd regularly taken turns dating him. Rumour had it they'd bet Theo's cousin, Benedict, a horse that Theo would never notice the difference. Rumour had it they'd won that bet. 'Letting your wife befriend your former mistresses?'

Theo's gaze sharpened. 'That would be very unwise. Good thing I claim no such intimacy with either Cordova twin. No, it's a simple matter of indulging my wife. Moriana finds them refreshing.'

Valentine snorted. He still thought putting the ruthlessly efficient Queen Consort Moriana together with the flagrantly wilful and rebellious Cordova twins was courting disaster. What if they decided to co-operate? They'd rule the world…or at the very least, this part of it. 'It's your catastrophe.'

'You have a quarrel with Angelique? Is that why you avoid her so diligently?'

'I don't avoid her.' He simply didn't go out of his way to encounter her. 'I have no quarrel with any of the Cordovas. They breed exceptionally fine horses and I envy your ability to get your hands on them.' The waiting list for a Cordova polo pony was ten years long. If you hailed from Thallasia, you were never going to get one.

'Your father wasn't exactly thinking ahead when

he banished Angelique from his stables all those years ago.'

Wrong. Valentine smiled tightly. His father had most definitely been thinking ahead.

'What was it for again? Riding your father's prize stallion without permission?'

'Racing my father's stallion against the fastest thoroughbred mare in the stables.' He should know. He'd been the one riding the mare.

'Your father also labelled her promiscuous, did he not?'

'Yes.' Another accusation Valentine had been partly, if not wholly, responsible for. 'My late father was not always right.' Nor was he missed by many, but that was not a thought Valentine cared to share aloud.

'And yet the accusation stuck,' Theo mused. 'A reputation Angelique decided to own rather than fight, because she knew from the beginning it was a fight she couldn't win. I respect her for that. So does my wife.' Theo turned on him. 'Do you ever wonder what she might have become without that black mark?'

'No.' He wanted to believe that Angelique was exactly who she wanted to be. 'Angelique Cordova is feted by polo players and royalty alike, owned by none, and beholden only unto herself. What's so bad about that?'

At times, he downright envied her.

They were leaning against a rail, sun on their

faces and a field full of polo ponies and riders in full view. They'd started out watching the play, although Valentine had abandoned that some time ago in favour of people-watching. If Angelique happened to be one of those people he studied more intently than others, so be it. With her ivory jodhpurs, knee-high black riding boots, fitted black shirt and her raven-black hair swept into a thick plait that started high on her head and finished at the swell of her magnificent rear, Angelique Cordova could command a dead man's attention. 'I'm thinking of renouncing my throne.'

Theo barely spared him a glance. 'Ha-ha.'

'I'm serious.' Theo's royal fields were a robust green, with woodland to one side and the white stone palace of Liesendaach behind them. It was a picture-perfect venue for the charity matches being played and later there would be a glittering ball to round out the day. Fat coffers would open, and at the end of the evening another hospital unit or education programme would be funded. Valentine had weathered a thousand days just like this one. He couldn't stomach the thought of a thousand more. 'I'm serious,' he repeated quietly.

Theo had turned to face him more fully, his expression sharply concerned. 'You can't be.'

And yet he was. 'You speak of that moment when Angelique was dismissed as if it were a turning point in her life. Something that shaped her world from that moment onwards. You speak as if she recognised it as such and embraced it, right or wrong. Angelique Cordova: passionate, headstrong and fallen.' He wondered if Theo had any idea just how much Valentine had wanted to turn his back on everything he'd been raised to do and run away with her. 'I too find myself at a turning point not entirely of my making. And, much like Angelique, I can either fight against these new circumstances and lose, or embrace them and see where it takes me. I'm tired, Theo.' And infertile now too, and therein lay the crux of the matter.

What use an infertile king?

'I know you've been ill, but my people tell me you're fully recovered.'

'You mean, that's what your spies tell you.'

'Were they *wrong*?'

Valentine huffed a laugh at the underlying thread of astonishment in Theo's voice. 'Surely it must happen from time to time, no?'

'No.' Theo glared at him. 'Are you dying?'

'No.'

'Losing your mind?'

'I gather you think it a possibility.'

'I do think it a possibility. And don't try and tell me you're mourning the loss of your perfectly serene fiancée because I won't believe you. She bored you stupid.'

'She enhanced my image.' It really had been as cold-blooded as that. 'She was perfectly pleasant.'

'And. Bored. You. Senseless. And setting aside

the possible reasons for your abdication, who would rule Thallasia if not you? Your sister? How can you possibly think that's a viable option?'

'Why not?'

Theo was silent for long seconds as if contemplating just such a future, and then, 'Your sister has many fine qualities but a leader she is not.'

'She can learn. I'll help her.'

'It's not a matter of learning, it's a matter of character.' Frustration lent weight to Theo's voice. 'Your sister is secure only in her beauty, which—while considerable—is already beginning to fade. Indecisiveness plagues her and always has. She's easily swayed by flattery. And for all that her husband loves her, he's not been built to provide the support a ruling queen needs. You want my opinion or you'd never have broached the subject with me in the first place. Listen as I give it. Your sister is not you. All the progress you've made—*we've* made—in the region these past few years since your father's death will be at risk. Is that what you want?'

'I think you underestimate my sister.' People always had.

'Why are you even thinking this?' asked Theo.

Again, Valentine had no answer for him. Funny how impossible it was to talk about the infertility that had resulted from his recent illness. Funny how his ability to sire children was so entwined with his role as King and his identity. Funny, not funny. 'I could still advise her.'

'Or you could remain King.' Theo's patience had reached its limit. 'I am a king. Born, bred and steeped in all that the role entails. So are you. We serve, like it or not. *Never* do we turn our back on crown and country. I don't know what else you want me to say.'

'Nothing. I want you to say nothing.'

'It would help if you actually told me what was behind your thinking. Because *"I'm tired"* is not exactly cutting it as an excuse for abdication!'

'It's all you're getting.' Valentine's temper itched to be unleashed, but on what he did not know. Theo was right in all he'd said. There was no way out of service for the likes of them. There never had been. And still anger rode him, played him in a way he hadn't allowed himself to be played in years, looking for an outlet, any outlet would do. 'And why on earth do you have amateurs playing with pros here today? I can't even watch this game without cursing the mess that number four is making of the play. Look at the way he's gouging his horse. How is this entertaining?' It wasn't. 'Who is he?'

'He's Europe's latest shipping billionaire, there's twenty seconds left on the clock, and if you'd been watching the game instead of Angelique you'd already know that both teams have deliberately kept him out of play for at least half the chukka. What's more, that's a Cordova pony he's attempting to ride. I fully expect that privilege to be revoked the moment he dismounts.'

The referee called time. The players left the field. The number four on the blue team rode to where Angelique stood waiting. Her shoulders formed a rigid frame, her hands rested on her hips, and even from here Valentine could tell she was livid. Angelique Cordova consumed by her emotions always had been a sight to behold.

Some things never changed.

'Do me a favour, since you've no quarrel with the Cordovas,' Theo challenged dulcetly. 'Get over there and give Angelique some backup. Europe's newest shipping billionaire didn't amass his vast wealth by being tolerant and kindly.'

'Why me? What are you going to do?'

'Me? I'm going to take the man's place on the polo field. Someone has to replace him in the next chukka and it may as well be me.'

'You're a terrible host. I don't know why I humour you.' But they'd already started walking towards the stables.

A flash of teeth and glinting grey eyes. 'I'll make it up to you.'

Leverage. How quaint. 'You certainly will.'

'I'll change your seating arrangements for dinner tonight, how's that?'

He already knew he was seated at the head of a table and across from Theo's current Minister for Agriculture—a happy man and an excellent raconteur. To his right would be the very married, very elderly, former Grand Duchess of the Opera—a woman whose golden voice had been surpassed only by her rapier wit. 'I like where I'm sitting tonight.' He'd already approved the new arrangements swapping his ex-fiancée out and the old Duchess in.

'Trust me—'

'Highly unlikely,' Valentine interrupted.

'—you'll like my seating arrangements more.'

If Angelique's raw beauty had been her downfall in her teens, by her late twenties she'd honed it into a dagger with which to pierce men's hearts. Lush lips in an otherwise finely drawn face. A body full of feminine strength and dangerous curves. Elegant black brows to accompany her masses of black hair. Flashing black eyes full of passion and pride. There was knowledge in her eyes when her gaze swept briefly over Valentine—knowledge of him—and so there should be.

She'd been his first.

And he'd been hers.

'Hello, Valentine. Whatever you want, it's going to have to wait,' she said as she turned back towards the horse and rider she was tending. The reins were in her hands now, not the billionaire's, and Valentine was of the firm belief that that was where they should stay. Up close he could see pink spittle around the horse's mouth and a skittishness about the pony that he was willing to bet hadn't been there seven minutes ago.

'Blood in my horse's mouth,' she muttered. 'Torn

skin from the gouging of your spurs.' She turned on the man. 'What were you trying to do? Gut the horse?'

The man puffed up: chest out and a sneer to go with it. 'Do you have anything more responsive?'

'Responsive to you? No.' Angelique eyed the man with undisguised disdain. 'I don't care how much money you paid to be here or who vouched for you—although, believe me, I will be having words with them—you will have no more horses from me. Not today. Not any day.'

'Keep your horse. It was no good anyway. Who's in charge here?'

'In charge of the horses on loan to visitors?' She was practically vibrating with anger. 'That would be me—Horsemaster Cordova—so let me repeat, I have no horses available for your next chukka, or the one after that, or the one after that. I have no horses available for your use, *ever*! I don't care if I am the only one willing to say it to your face. *You can't ride.*'

For a moment, Valentine thought the man might well take his hand to her, but did she back down? No.

She stepped up into the man's space, all five feet five of her to his substantially taller frame. 'Do it,' she murmured. 'See what happens when you strike *me.*'

A challenge that was more than enough incentive for Valentine to step up and put Angelique behind him. 'Problems?' he asked with a quiet menace of his own.

The man backed down, still livid but no longer within striking distance of either Angelique or the horse.

'I've heard of her and her family,' the man said with an ugly smirk. 'Her father's the one in charge of the horses, not her. She's just the whore. And he will hear of this.'

Valentine could have told him not to waste his breath. Cross one Cordova and you crossed them all. The man didn't know it yet, but he'd just been black-listed by the family that provided horses to half of Europe's elite. 'I'm sure he will, but here's what you need to remember. There were seven other players out on that field and let's not forget the spectators. And while bad sportsmanship is tolerated on occasion, bad horsemanship is unforgivable. It's exactly as the lady says. That was your first and last ride on a Cordova horse. Nor will you find any other horses available for your use here today.'

'Says who?'

'Ah. Of course. Allow me to introduce myself. King Valentine of Thallasia, sent by your host King Theodosius of Liesendaach, with the message that he has the sudden urge to play the next chukka in the number four position for the blue team. Kings and their whims, what can you do?'

'I know what you could both do,' muttered Angelique, waving a dismissive hand in Valentine's direction. '*You* could go back to being swooned over by your adoring sycophants. *He* could take up golf instead of polo. No horses involved. Just egos and little balls to smack around.'

Valentine watched as the man took his exit without another word. When he turned back to the horse, the bridle was gone and so too was the saddle, both of them unceremoniously dumped in a pile on the floor. The horse stood there, unbound and quivering as Angelique soothed it with her touch and crooned soft reassurances in Spanish. She had a way with wild things.

They probably recognised a kindred spirit.

'C'mon, let's cool her down.' Cool you down too, but at least he had the sense not to say as much aloud. 'Let's walk.'

She walked towards a vacant stall and the horse walked with her. She took the halter hanging from a peg next to the stall and put it on the horse and then they walked some more. No lead rein, she didn't need one. The horse followed, trusting her judgement, her presence, the hand she kept on its neck.

'What do you want, Your Majesty?' she finally asked without looking at him. 'Why are you still here?'

'You called me by my name earlier.'

'I forgot my place. Please accept my humble apologies.'

'Humble? Hardly.' Angelique Cordova was many

things. Humble was not one of them. 'You made an enemy just now.'

She shrugged. 'I said what I had to say.'

'Oh, I think you said a little more than that.' Scorn was a powerful blade and she'd used it without mercy. 'He's a powerful man.'

'They usually are.' She led the pony to the wash area and turned on the hose. 'Are you just going to stand there, or do you plan to be of use?'

He didn't move to hold the horse or take the hose. There were halter clips hanging there if she wished to secure the animal and he knew better than to try and take charge of a horse in Angelique's care. 'I was of use. My presence prevented him from striking you.'

'Maybe.' She seemed wholly unconcerned by the notion. 'I'll mention your belated chivalry to my father. He still has a tendency to curse your existence.'

'You do that.' He should leave now. 'Maybe I'll be forgiven.'

'Don't count on it.'

And there was the rub. Yes, he'd screwed up. He'd been so young at the time and he'd followed his heart, lost it, and been punished accordingly. Could *no one* cut him any slack? 'You were of age, Angelique. And more than willing.'

'I was. And had our obsession with each other been allowed to fade on its own as these things inevitably do, I would have remembered you fondly. As it was, your father stepped in with his baseless accusations and instant dismissal and you didn't fight for me or my honour, not one little bit. You took my gift and then broke my heart and the world moved on. I'd thank you for defending my honour here today only you're a dozen years too late.'

She didn't look at him as she allowed the pony to drink from the hose.

'What makes you think I didn't speak up for you?'

She didn't answer.

'Angelique, what exactly did you think was going to happen? Did you expect us to marry?'

'No.' She scowled at nothing in particular. 'But you let them say those things about me. You let me wear the shame, and for that I don't forgive you.'

'You have no idea what was said behind closed doors.' He'd tried desperately to take the blame. Told his father that none of it was Angelique's fault, that she shouldn't be dismissed on account of his bad judgement, and it had made not a scrap of difference to the way she and her family had been treated. As for him, he'd been whipped until he bled and charged with four years of military service for his trouble, and it hadn't been because he'd bedded the stable girl.

He'd been punished for *defending* her.

Not only had his skin split, so too had his heart when he'd realised that all Vala's dire warnings about their father being a petty tyrant had been true. Cruelty ruled the man. Cruelty, indifference to the plight of others and a soaring sense of entitlement, the last of which Valentine knew he shared.

Angelique might not know it but she'd saved him that day. Ripped the blinkers from his eyes, caused him to examine the privileges he'd taken for granted, and ultimately set him on a path of self-discovery that led him far from his father's cruel shadow.

Even if he did still have a way to go. 'My father gave me two choices on the day he stepped in to put a stop to our dalliance. The first was to let you go. The second was for him to taste what you'd so willingly given me. Would you rather I'd kept you at his mercy? Because I'm telling you, Angelique, just in case you missed the memo. My father was not a pleasant man.'

All the anger that had simmered beneath his skin for years finally broke the surface. The years of being treated like a fiend by her and her family. The judgment his peers had applied to their affair, Theo's thinly veiled criticism. The guilt he carried with him still when it came to the position he'd put her in all those years ago. The thanks he owed her that she didn't want to hear.

The way he wanted her, still. After all those years spent trying to forget the feel of her heart thundering against his and never, ever being able to actually do so.

Anger, sharp and corrosive, was such an old, old friend.

'Take heart from your escape from the royal court

of Thallasia, Horsemaster Cordova. Thank your lucky stars I thought enough of you to let you go. You got to be free. You got to be you. It could have been so much worse.' His heels came together in a parody of a military-parade-ground salute and he smiled bleakly and bowed his farewell. 'You could have stayed.'

CHAPTER TWO

'I'M NOT GOING.' Angelique Cordova stared at her twin sister and tried to push down the panic that threatened to overwhelm her. The charity dinner scheduled to begin in an hour would go ahead without her. She could stay right where she was in the pretty blue and bronze guest room of the living quarters Prince Benedict shared with her brother Carlos. They'd been together openly for over a year now, with both Benedict and Carlos taking up residence in Theo's palace. They wouldn't mind if she hid out in their apartment and it wasn't as if she'd be missed at the ball. There were five hundred other people attending, most of them rich, many of them titled, plenty of them self-absorbed. They could pretend interest in each other while she stayed here and unwound. She turned towards her sister, willing her to understand. 'I can't do it.'

Luciana stared back at her, almost identical in looks but for a slightly deeper dimple when she smiled and a crooked pinkie finger courtesy of a bad break when she was a child.

'I could say I'm ill. Exhausted from the events of the day. Which I am.'

'Liar.' Lucia surveyed her solemnly. 'This is about your temperamental King of Thallasia—'

'He's not my King.'

'—and the run-in you had with him earlier.'

'How did you hear about that?'

'Everyone's heard about it. He breaks his engagement in the morning and by lunchtime he's sniffing after you and dredging up the good old days when our name was mud and no one wanted anything to do with us.'

'I hate to break it to you, but our name is still mud.' Even their brother's outing as Prince Benedict of Liesendaach's live-in lover hadn't helped. 'We're just well-connected mud now.'

'Yes, we are, and I for one would like to remain so. You can't let Valentine get to you. He's nothing to you now. A past lover. If he approaches you, turn him down.'

'I don't want to be near him.' It didn't seem to matter how many years had passed. All he had to do was look at her, be in the same room as her, and her heart started trying to crawl out of her chest and make its way towards him. 'I'm still affected by him. And now he's single and looking straight at me so I can't be around him. Lucia, please, can't we do a sister swap? You can pretend to be me and just…insult him…until he goes away. You're better at it than me.'

'Only because I've never forgiven him for the state he left you in all those years ago, whereas you…your heart is too soft and your memory not nearly long enough. No. I know your vulnerability when it comes to the Thallasian King as well as you do, but like it or not you have to find a way to deal with him that doesn't involve making yourself scarce every time he appears.'

'He came to my defence today.' She'd appreciated it more than she'd let on. 'It was unexpected.'

Lucia looked wholly unimpressed. 'You don't need defending.'

'I know. It's just—'

'It's just nothing. So he's not a complete waste of a man. Doesn't matter. You can't let him back into your life—he'll use you as a rebound fling to get over his broken engagement and then marry a dutiful princess. You *know* this. The world at large knows this, and you are not going to play that game. You need to put on your gown and the diamond necklace and earrings that go with it and go out there tonight and be pleasantly indifferent to him should he seek you out.'

Angelique met her sister's gaze in the mirror that ran the full length of the dressing room.

'He's just a man,' her sister said softly. 'A man who once held your heart, but you've taken it back and moved on. You're here at the invitation of a king and his Queen. You had a job to do today and you did it and I heard only praise for you and our horses. So what if Valentine of Thallasia came to your defence? Too little, too late and what's more you don't need his patronage. Let him see you in all your strength and glory. Hell, let him *want* what he so carelessly threw away. Doesn't mean he'll get it.'

Her sister sounded so *sure*.

'He said I had a lucky escape from him and his family.' He'd said it with such bitter conviction.

Her sister moved to drape the diamond necklace over Angelique's collarbones. 'Dear heart, believe him.'

When Theo had promised to change Valentine's dinner seating arrangements for the better, Valentine had stupidly not seen those words for a threat. Banquet seating was a fine art and Theo's wife, Moriana, was the best of the best when it came to seating people to their advantage. The arrangements had been thrown out on account of his ex's departure earlier that morning, but it had been sorted not half an hour later when the Grand Dame of Opera had stepped in to take her place. He truly hadn't thought Theo's threat worth worrying about.

But it wasn't the Grand Dame of Opera who slipped into the seat beside him and turned an almost faultless smile in his direction several minutes later.

Nor was it Angelique.

It was her sister.

'Luciana,' he greeted, not the slightest bit tempted to use her shorter nickname. Angelique's twin had never hidden her utter contempt for him. Loyal to the last. A part of him had always admired that about her. 'Stunning as always.'

'I am, rather,' she murmured. 'And you...' her eyes raked him from ceremonial head to toe, and then she shrugged '...too. All those sashes and impressive little medals on your breast.'

'Chest,' he corrected. 'You have a breast. I have a chest. Would you like some wine?'

No sooner had he said it than a waiter appeared, but she waved him away with a murmur of thanks and then a no. 'You can be sure that once the evening is over, I'll be heading for my brother's finest wine. Until then, no. I have far too many people to watch over this evening to be doing so with a cloudy mind. And while we're on the subject of clear minds, how is it that you always know I'm not my sister?'

'Magic.' In all honesty, he had no idea how he could so easily tell one from another. But he could.

'Better that than saying you imprinted on her young and have never been able to wash the essence of her from your soul, I suppose.'

'Much better. And not nearly as bloodthirsty.'

'Still. My version's more romantic.'

'In what universe are you a romantic?' Not that he meant to be rude...

'Oh, okay. I'm a ball-breaker.'

That she was. Luciana might not have always had

Angelique's tarnished reputation to contend with. People had painted her as the good sister for many years, right up until she'd become the mistress of a married nobleman and then refused to marry him once he was free. Once a cheat, always a cheat, she'd declared, and moved on without a backward glance. Moved on to parties with movie stars and billionaires, princelings and sportsmen and cut a swathe through them all. These days, Luciana's reputation rivalled her sister's. And Theo's court was their new playing field. 'Why are you here?'

'Sisterly love. The seating arrangements were changed at the very last minute, as I'm sure you were aware.' She stopped speaking to regard him more intently. 'Oh. You weren't aware. That's *very* interesting. Anyway, where was I?'

Did the dippy act *ever* work for her? He thought not. 'You were speaking of Angelique.'

'Yes, of course I was. You and your obsessions. It's almost quaint the way you've never forgotten her. Angelique was up before dawn and has spent all day pandering to entitled aristocrats who take one look at her and think she'd like to end the day naked beneath them. She in turn took one look at the changes to tonight's seating arrangement—which seated her next to you—and said, "I have shovelled more excrement today than any being can be expected to shovel in a day and none of it has come from the rear end of a horse. I can't do this. I'm too tired."' Luciana beamed. 'And so here I am.'

Charming. 'And your host knows about this swap?'

Luciana shrugged. 'Theo does not—in fact—know everything. A disappointment he struggles to contain, I know, but that's just the way it is.'

'You're funny.'

'Oh, stop with your flirting before I castrate you.'

He'd rather flirt with an angry lioness. 'And people wonder why the Cordova twins are still single.'

'No one *I* know wonders that,' she said, dry as dust. 'Do keep up.'

'Still funny.' But he could barely bring himself to be amused. That Angelique had taken one look at the seating arrangements and decided she couldn't abide to be anywhere near him filled him with a strange restlessness. Their earlier encounter had left him wanting…something. Absolution, forgiveness, a spectacular argument—any of that would do. He had bitterness to burn and Angelique had never been one to shirk from confrontation. The stoking of old embers—that too might satisfy.

What was it Angelique had said earlier? *If their attraction had been allowed to run its course, it would be done and dusted by now.* Or words to that effect. But it hadn't, and it wasn't, and maybe it *was* time to explore what they'd started all those years ago. Put it properly to bed. He needed no royal wife any more, no paragon of virtue and mother to his children. Why *not* pick up with Angelique where they'd left off and see where it took them?

He stood and studied the half-dozen long tables set up in a banquet hall that sparkled and shone the way only a Liesendaach banquet hall could. He spotted Angelique at the other side of the room, seated with Benedict and her brother and a professional polo player whose on-field play he liked a whole lot more than the easy smile the man was sharing with Angelique. 'Ah. There she is.' He turned to her sister. 'And here you are, and, as diverting as our conversation is, it's time you returned to your designated seat and let Angelique take hers. Shall you send her over or will I collect her?'

But Luciana had been forced to stand when he had, and her drawling ennui looked to have been replaced by temper, fierce and somewhat familiar. 'I'll be nice,' she said through gritted teeth. 'I'll be positively delightful. Baiting you is boring anyway. And in return you're going to leave my sister be.'

'No. That's not going to work for me. I'm feeling reckless, you see.' Reckless, cornered and somewhat defeated. It wasn't a good combination. He bowed like the good little Courtier King he was. 'Get a move on, Luciana, and send your sister to me. You're in the wrong seat.'

She left without further comment.

CHAPTER THREE

ANGELIQUE WATCHED FROM afar as Queen Consort Moriana waylaid the grumpy King of Thallasia. Valentine was ready to leave, anyone with a discerning eye could see that. She spared a glance for Luciana, who was gliding back towards the seat Angelique currently occupied. So much for the last-minute sister-swap agreement. Angelique hastily excused herself and rose to meet Lucia halfway. As always, they drew glances, especially once they stood together. Heated gazes grew longer and more covetous as she and Lucia became *those* women—the beautiful, untameable Cordova twins with their Spanish blood and fierce tempers and faces that could make poets weep. Scorned by most women and desired by so many men, and she was used to it, had taken the stereotype imprinted on her and turned it into a weapon. But God help her she was tired of wielding it. 'What happened?'

'Your handsome King is in a very bad mood.

Being denied what he wants doesn't seem to agree with him.'

'What does he want?'

'You. And I don't think running away is going to do anything but rouse his hunting instinct. You need to shut him down, turn him away, and there is no time like now. Come, we shall both walk over and pretend to be up to our old twin tricks again. We shall be infamous for daring to fool yet another king, and then I shall draw the lovely Moriana away and you'll take your seat and be charmingly indifferent. And then we'll go home and rethink how invested in Carlos' new world we want to be. I for one could use a change of scenery.' She bared her teeth at a nearby ogler. 'Keep your eyes in your head, Grandpa. You can't afford us.'

'That's *definitely* not going to help,' murmured Angelique as she steered her sister away from the old man's impending apoplexy. It took a while for her and Lucia to reach their targets. Along the way they collected a retired opera star who couldn't wear enough diamonds to fully cover her papered, wrinkly flesh, but by heaven she tried, and Angelique respected that. And then somehow the opera Grand Dame, Queen Consort Moriana, Lucia and Angelique all ended up in a standing circle with a glowering Valentine, while they peppered the space with smiles and laughter and airy greetings. Social lubrication at its finest.

'Finally, my seat,' she said to the older man standing awkwardly across the table from her. 'I was quite caught up on the other side of the room until my sister came for me.'

'He knows you're lying.' It was Valentine's voice in her ear. Valentine who pulled out her chair and then deliberately seated himself, forcing all those around him to sit. 'He's simply too polite to say so.'

The others wandered away, still mingling, bright birds picking up scattered seed, and it was well done, the social efforts that had detained a king and allowed him time to settle once more to the part expected of him.

He turned to study her, his gaze an almost tangible press against her soul and skin. 'I didn't think you'd come.'

'Well, you were about to leave before the meal had even begun. I could have been blamed, as I so often am when there's a scandal in the making. And rather than see all my fine work infiltrating Theo's court go to waste, I decided to co-operate. So here I am. Honoured to be dining at your side. I'll try to remember to use the right fork.'

He hurt her eyes with all his finery. The medals. The sash. And on his finger a heavy-looking gold ring that she'd never seen up close. The royal signet ring of Thallasia, once worn by his father and now worn by him.

The King.

His face was formidable, not a trace of the boy she'd once known so well in the hard planes of his cheek and jaw. No sign of laughter in his fathomless black eyes. But then, rumour had it he had little to smile about. 'I hear you no longer have a fiancée— is that true?'

'Correct.'

'My condolences.' Nope, she didn't sound even the slightest bit sincere, and his raised eyebrow told her he'd clocked it too. Jealousy was a chore, but in for a penny... 'The two of you were so photogenic together. All her pale, aristocratic reserve and your brutal indifference. Who'd have thought it wouldn't last?'

His eyes glinted pure and heady challenge. 'I'm sure some of us must have had our doubts. But enough about me. Are you seeing anyone?'

'Several someones, as always.' Never mind that her workday reality begged to differ. She saw a lot of people every day. And dated none of them.

'Name them. Or do you prefer them married, and are thus unable to speak their names?'

'No, you're thinking of Lucia. I prefer them generous, open, and laughing.' She paused while a waiter whisked away the half-filled water glass in front of her and a full one took its place. The moment he left, another attendant offered wine. She chose the white and murmured her thanks. 'I also prefer them not ashamed to be seen with me. Guess that rules you out.'

'Not at all.' He leaned back in his chair, his at-

tention all for her. 'We're here in public right now.
And there are many eyes upon us.'

'Probably because you want to make a new headline to overshadow your failed engagement and broken heart. And while I'm sure our salacious past
and my wild reputation could help you there, I'm
not feeling generous enough to accommodate you.
I have no taste for the public feeding frenzy that
would descend once you cast me aside. Again.'

'I might keep you this time.'

'You couldn't afford me.'

He countered with a look that suggested he could
probably afford just about anything. 'You never
know. What is it you want?'

'Your heart in my hands, bloody and dripping.'

'Ah.' He almost smiled. 'Revenge. I can work
with that.'

'No, you can't. And as flattered as I am to have
been seated next to you this evening—was that your
idea?'

'Theo's.'

'Right.' So Valentine had been blindsided by the
change to the seating plans as well. 'So, King Theodosius thought to seat you next to the one person
you don't want to spend time with. Are you feud-
ing with him?'

'Not yet. I rather think our host thought he was
helping. He wants us to make amends.'

'And you? What do you want?'

His long, strong fingers toyed with the stem of

his wine glass, and then he downed the drink in one go. Not the action of a king who could generally be counted on to make a glass of wine last all night. Not that she knew such things about him. Not that she'd been watching him from afar for years.

She looked at him, really looked at him. The shadows beneath his eyes that spoke of too little sleep, the tension lines bracketing his mouth, and as for his eyes themselves, the inky brown-black of them, they held an emptiness she'd never seen in him before. Maybe he *had* cared for his former fiancée more than he'd ever let on. She hated that thought but couldn't discount it. 'I don't want to give you the impression of caring one way or another, but are you all right? Because you seem a little…off.'

'Off?'

'Unwell. Out of sorts. It's like…you don't seem yourself.'

He smiled, but it did not reach his eyes. 'Because you know me so well.'

She had once. She'd swum in his soul and he knew it. He was the first to look away. The first to start a conversation with the man seated opposite him. She reached for her drink and turned to introduce herself to the young gentleman on her other side. She could do this. Make light of her unease, turn away from him with every evidence of civility. No drinking in every little thing about him or worrying about what tomorrow would bring.

There would be no better way to have his adoring public think he was careening wildly towards the edge of sanity than for him to pursue her again.

He *knew* this, surely.

The meal came and went. Angelique didn't slurp her soup, drop her fork or start an argument. Doubtless, some people were disappointed. Instead, she talked with a Minister of Agriculture about water rights, and chatted with the young man next to her about horses—Cordova horses specifically—and the very long waiting list for one. At some point she might have been goaded into offering Valentine the use of a polo pony for the weekend's festivities, should he choose to ride. She drank very little and tried not to pay attention to Valentine's every movement. She shifted restlessly beneath the prick of borrowed jewels at her neck and the agony of time passing too slowly. She wanted nothing more than to go and check on her horses—horses that were already magnificently stabled and in the care of grooms who knew what they were doing—but the dancing was about to begin and she *knew* what she needed to do next, and that was dance with Valentine and feign indifference and then leave him to get on with whatever existential crisis he was having.

Because it was quite apparent to her and plenty of others that he was having one.

She turned to find him studying her. Again. 'Is my face not to your liking?'

'I like it better without the make-up, yes.'

'I always wear make-up.' Coloured sun-protection

cream at the very least. Protective gloss for her lips. Her eyelashes were thick and dark and rarely needed mascara, though, and physical labour throughout the day tended to bring warm colour to her cheeks.

'Then I like you better with less.'

'I suspect this is simply a setting you've never pictured me in before.'

'Angelique, I say with complete confidence that I've pictured you in practically every setting imaginable. And you have always conquered it.'

Oh. Well. That was very… 'Kind of you,' she murmured.

'What are your thoughts on children?' he asked next, and she blinked.

'Are you usually all over the place with your conversation?' Because she hadn't remembered that about him.

'Humour me.'

'I really, really am.'

'Then what are your thoughts on having children?' he repeated.

'I don't have any children. You might have noticed.' Not that she didn't want to be a mother one day, maybe, but a relationship with someone special came first. A marriage the likes of which her parents had. Not dull, never that, but strongly nurturing, loving and secure. And *that* kind of relationship had never happened her way. 'What about you? Regretting the loss of your fiancée already? You should have married her earlier. Got some little heirs on the ground, created your happy family. Of course, you're still young so your lack of children isn't such a problem. Take your time.'

He smiled grimly. 'You're being obnoxious.'

Better he thought her obnoxious than overly sensitive, defensive and way out of her comfort zone. 'I haven't deliberately spilled anything on you yet and caused an outrage. *I* think I'm being very restrained. That's because I'm worried about you.'

'Dance with me.' It wasn't a request.

'You really want that headline tomorrow, don't you? The one saying you've lost your mind and are once again consorting with the help.'

'I want nothing of the kind. Doesn't change the fact that I'll get it anyway. May as well go big.'

'You *are* bitter.'

'Don't forget twisted. Either dance with me or walk away, Angelique. Either way it'll make the news. You know that as well as I do.'

There was no humour in him. None. And again, concern for him plagued her. 'What happened to you?'

'I grew up. I'm growing old waiting to see if you'll dance with me, as is customary given the seating arrangements imposed on us.'

'One dance and done?'

'One and done. If that's what you want.'

'What else would I want?'

So many eyes on them as she placed her hand on the sleeve of his dress jacket and allowed him to escort her onto the dance floor. By tomorrow the gossip columns would be full of stories about the Thallasian King, his broken engagement, and his childhood whore—that would be her—but she couldn't care about that right now. All she cared about was making it through this dance without getting carried away by his nearness and his touch.

Some people danced stiffly or clumsily with one another. Some never quite meshed, unable to truly sink into the moment and just let go.

That had never been their problem.

His hand at her waist, warm and possessive. Her hand on his shoulder—no shoulder pads for him, just the seeping warmth of his skin beneath the finest of cloth. The brush of his hips, the huff of his breath against her hair as he dipped his head towards hers and they began to move. They'd never danced like this before, not formally, in a ballroom.

And still, it felt as if they'd already done it a thousand times over.

'I've missed you,' he murmured, and she faltered in her steps, causing him to step in closer to steady her. 'My greatest fear has always been that no other woman would ever satisfy me the way you did.'

'But they have.' She tried to sound confident. 'I'm sure.'

'Don't be so sure.' His fingers tightened fractionally around hers and his cheek brushed hers. She could have sworn her heart was beating in time with his. 'Want to run away with me, Angelique, while I turn my back on my family, my duty and my country?'

'Don't be stupid.' But when she looked him in the eyes, she didn't see a man who'd spoken teasing words. All she saw was a man in the deepest, darkest despair. 'What's wrong?' She might not have spoken to him in years, but she'd watched him from afar and she could still pick up on his moods, heaven help her she could. 'What's going on?'

A touch of concern, the slightest bit of care. Angelique in his arms again and he was ready to spill all his secret hopes and fears. Same as he'd done all those years ago amongst the hay in the feed loft or the shadows of a stable door. They'd grown closer while dancing, because together they became magnetic. Spin one way and they would repel each other. Spin them the other and they became as one.

He was a breath away from crushing her lips beneath his, and only a lifetime of having courtly protocols beaten into him kept him in check. 'I want to see you again.'

He wanted his hands on her and hers on him and the thought that she didn't seem to want children shouldn't have buoyed him as much as it did. But what if? What if he *could* now have this with her?

She stared at him as if searching for a catch. 'Why now? Why, after a dozen years, am I suddenly of interest to you? Nothing has changed. You're a king. I'm still me. And if you think I can't tell there's something else going on with you, you are sadly mistaken.'

She was too perceptive. Could read his moods better than he knew them himself. 'I'm a free man and I'd like to get to know you again. Which part don't you understand?' The dancing spun to an end and Angelique stepped away, out of his arms with insulting swiftness.

'I don't understand any of it. And the answer's no. You don't know me. You never did.'

'Your favourite wine was Spanish white, your favourite meal your mother's seafood rice, and your father was the best horseman you'd ever seen and probably still is. I know what you told me, what you showed me back then. It was a gift I've not forgotten.'

'You don't smile any more,' was what she said.

She could help with that. But first she had to want what he offered and nothing about her behaviour tonight suggested she did. Manners carried Valentine to the completion of their farce as he escorted her to the sidelines of the dance floor, bowed and took his leave. Let the gossip-mongers talk as he headed for the exit and the privacy of his guest rooms. Let him be taken to task for not dancing with other, more acceptable women. Let them say he was in thrall once more to the stable hand.

He didn't care.

CHAPTER FOUR

'DID YOU SEE THIS?' Angelique's brother, Carlos, sat in the courtyard of the royal quarters he shared with Prince Benedict of Liesendaach. Their quarters were situated on the ground floor of the west wing of the royal palace. Given that Angelique had been up with the dawn to tend polo ponies and was only now returning for breakfast, it was a fair call to say she had no idea what her brother was talking about.

'What is it you want me to see?'

'Thallasia's national newspaper. Front page. Above the fold.'

'And?' She leaned over his shoulder and plucked a sweet roll from the basket. No need for butter; she liked them plain and warm and slightly sticky on top and the kitchen here did not disappoint.'

'"Scandal Rocks the Thallasian Throne as King Valentine Threatens to Quit."'

'What?' She almost choked on her roll.

'It mentions you too.'

'It does not!'

'Yes, you were seen having a spirited conversation with him in the stables.'

'Ah. Well, yes.'

'And again during the banquet.'

'That was very cordial.'

'Cosy was the word used. And then there was the dancing.'

'It was *one* dance.'

'Shockingly intimate, I think you'll find, and then he left and then you left—'

'To tend the horses. As many, *many* people can confirm.' She reached for the coffee pot and hoped the coffee in it was sufficiently strong and hot. 'Why's he threatening to quit the throne?'

'Oh, that's your fault too. His people won't accept you as his Queen—'

'True enough.'

'—and you've given him an ultimatum. Make an honest woman of you or your rekindled romance is dead.'

Angelique sighed. 'So much for being able to do my job today with *that* rumour flying around.'

'Unless, of course, you consider it your job to bring about the downfall of kings.' Carlos sipped his coffee and kept on reading. 'There's a quote from a billionaire.'

'Oh, you mean the one who can't ride?'

'The very one. He fears for Valentine's mental health, what with being in thrall to a shrew like you.'

'I'm never going to be invited back here again,

am I? They're going to say, *"By all means bring
your Cordova ponies to the picnic, but please leave
that king-slaying shrew behind."* Father's going to
ask me how this went and I'm going to have to say
I've stuffed it up again. It wasn't my fault but, hey,
who cares?'

'It's not that bad.'

'Speak for *yourself*, Carlos. It's bad enough.'

Carlos regarded her patiently. 'Why don't you
give an interview?' He gestured towards the paper.
'Set things straight.'

'Because no one wants to *hear* my side of the
story. People want the scandal, not the truth.' She
nibbled on her suddenly tasteless breakfast roll and
her brother silently pushed a bowl of marmalade in
her direction. She had a sweet tooth when stressed.
She ripped her roll in half and slathered a generous
supply of marmalade on both halves before jam-
ming it back together again. 'Last night's civility
was supposed to *fix* things, not stir all those old
stories up again.'

'It's possible we miscalculated.'

'Oh, *you think*?'

Carlos regarded her steadily. 'I'll help you with
the horses today. That'll shield you from the worst
of it.'

'I'll let Lucia know to brace herself. Maybe she
can wear a name tag.'

'She would never.' Carlos smiled fondly. 'We're
Cordovas. Family solidarity is our strength.'

She nodded and rubbed at her temple with the heel of her palm. 'I told Valentine he could ride our horses today.'

'Why on earth did you tell him that?'

'Because I'm weak and pitiful and thought it might help. Nothing to see here, no feuds of old. Just regular people going about their business. Wonder if I can take it back?' But she knew she wouldn't, just as she knew Valentine would ride a Cordova horse today regardless of the hatchet job they'd done on him in the press, or maybe because of it. It was a matter of pride.

'There's one more thing they're speculating about in this article.'

'What *now*?' But the sudden rough gravity in her brother's voice made her uneasy.

'Not about you. It's about Valentine and his recent illness.'

She didn't even know he'd been ill, but it explained a lot.

'They're saying it made him infertile.'

'They're saying *what*?'

'No children for the King of Thallasia. No direct heirs. No need for him to take a wife or even for him to stay in power. He may step down.'

Suddenly Valentine's behaviour of yesterday and last night began to make sense. His reckless defiance. His interest in *her*. He didn't need to marry well any more. If he couldn't sire children, he didn't need to marry at all... 'That ratfink bastard!'

Her brother's eyebrows rose. 'Not quite the reaction I was expecting.'

'He's going slumming.' She waved the hand with her sweet roll in the air to emphasise her point. 'Sniffing around me all of a sudden because he's got it in his head he's only half a man now and no respectable woman will want him. Why *not* have me now, after all these years? He has nothing to lose!'

'To be fair, his thought process might be a little more nuanced than that.'

'All last night I worried about him.' Carlos was giving the man way too much credit. 'Twice, I asked him what was wrong, *three* times, but did he answer me? No. He couldn't even give me honesty! She waved her food in her brother's face and he leaned back and gently pushed it sideways. 'I'm going to castrate him.'

'Don't threaten with your food. Also, if this report is to be believed, he's already been unmanned. Give him a break.'

'You do *not* get to take his side in this.' Maybe she would want to eat her roll eventually, but as of this moment she'd quite lost her appetite. 'I'm right and he's an imbecile who can't come to terms with his new world order and is feeling *sorry* for himself. Boo hoo!'

'Are you done?'

'Would you like me to continue?' Because she could. 'Spoilt, self-obsessed, delusional, irritating…' *Hurting…* 'Don't you dare tell me he's not.'

'I wouldn't dream of it.' Anyone would think Carlos was used to such outbursts from her and knew exactly how to slide his way around them. 'But are we letting him on a horse?'

If there was one thing a man could count on in this world, it was Cordova family solidarity, decided Valentine as he stepped inside Theo's royal stables and headed for the Cordova horses. Carlos and Luciana had both joined Angelique in tending to their mounts today; preparing them for riders, making them look like the wildly expensive animals they doubtless were.

Carlos was point man, by the look of things, meaning anyone waiting for a horse dealt with him. Angelique and Luciana stayed in the background, glamorous and unattainable as they readied the animals for handover. Didn't matter to Valentine if he had to wait to be served, like everyone else. Didn't matter if Angelique had glared at him when he'd first arrived and then ignored him. He was here for Cordova horses to play polo on, because last night she'd made that offer and he was damned if he'd let his country's gutter press bleed every last vestige of pleasure from his existence.

'Angelique,' Carlos barked. 'Get the King's horse.'

Guess they weren't intending to keep him standing in line after all.

Carlos sent him a measuring stare and then ges-

tured with his head for Valentine to pass through
the invisible line Carlos had so effectively drawn to
keep people away from his sisters. 'You're getting
our very best today. All of them are bred for endur-
ance, agility and speed, but these ones are special.
Fit for a king.' Fine words, when every line in the
other man's body conveyed a very different message.
Screw this up and we're done. 'Interesting article in
the paper this morning.'

'You read that?' Who was he trying to fool? Everyone he'd met so far this morning had read the salacious 'interview'. Interview with whom? Not him.
Not Theo, the other King had been quick to inform
him. No, the piece had the air of an article that had
been a while in the making, with the distinct sniff
of leaks from his own court. His personal secretary had his suspicions and had already set a trap.
It wasn't the first time someone in his inner circle
had chosen money over honour. It wouldn't be the
last. The billionaire shipping magnate's quote had
been nothing more than an opportunistic addition.

'Any of it true?' asked Carlos, and at least the
man was blunt about it.

'The bit about your sister being a good horse-
woman is true.' Valentine supposed more openness
wouldn't go amiss at this point but he still couldn't
bring himself to address other parts of the interview
or clarify their truth. 'My apologies for bringing
your family under scrutiny again.'

'We're used to it.'

'Doesn't mean you have to like it.'

'Can't imagine you like it much either.' Carlos shrugged. A tall, wiry man, he had the beauty of face for which the Cordovas were famed and an air of calm that his sisters definitely lacked. Given that he'd taken up with Benedict, Prince of Liesendaach, and yet another temperamental diva, Valentine had to assume that other people's fireworks bothered him not. 'Angelique's convinced that if she gives you her mare to ride you'll score a dozen goals and show everyone you're more than the sum of that interview. Then she's going to rip you a new one for not being honest with her about your problems.'

The other man's words set Valentine back some. There was a lot to unpack and no time to do it in. 'I have no problems.'

'Ride well, Your Majesty.'

Angelique met him halfway across the stable yard, a stunning grey mare walking alongside her. The horse had keen, intelligent eyes and stood ready to ride. 'This is Armonía,' she said by way of greeting. 'It means Harmony in Spanish. She's fast on the turn and fearless when riding to the shoulder. She'll play best at number two, but so do you. I think you'll do well together.'

'Your brother says you're angry with me.' She met his gaze and smiled, tight and hard. 'It wasn't my intention to put you in the headlines again.'

'I couldn't care less what they say about me. Is it true you can no longer sire children?'

He nodded, just once. Which was more than anyone else had got from him on the subject.

'Do you have sperm frozen somewhere that you can use? Semen straws like we do for horses?'

'I'm not a horse, Angel. And, no, I put nothing aside. My mistake.'

'Could you adopt a child?'

'No.' He was a king, with all that his royal bloodline entailed. Why raise a child to understand the monarchy when they could never fully be part of it? 'I'm not that cruel.' Fatherhood of any kind was beyond him now. He was dealing with it. Not well, but still. 'If you pity me, I will never forgive you.'

'Why would I pity you? You're still a king, with access to untold wealth and resources. Still prettier than every other man here.' She waved an arm around as if to reduce all others in the vicinity to nothing. 'Still sexually functional—' his eyebrows rose '—I assume. Still desired by many, many women who would become your Queen and forgo having children. Still an ass, but let's not go there. I can be an ass too, given that I thought for a while that you might be turning your attentions to me once more because you figured you'd fallen so far in everyone's estimation why *not* consort with the help? Then I realised you hadn't actually *made* a move on me last night and then I got angry all over again because I couldn't tempt you, even when you were feeling unworthy. You can see my dilemma.'

'Er…'

'You can't see my dilemma? Probably for the best.' Her smile mocked him.

'About the horse…'

'Ah, yes. She needs to warm up. You need to get used to her. I suggest you check your towering self-pity at the door and get on with it. You *can* still ride, can't you?'

'What *towering self-pity*?'

'You can't see it? Rest assured, everyone else can. Tell your detractors to eat dirt and that you're staying on the throne because you're brilliant at what you do. Tell your people your twin sister has several children and the royal bloodline is secure and the necessary changes will be made as to who will rule next. And then love as you will.'

If only everything were that simple. 'You'd make a terrible royal adviser.'

She tossed her head, a picture of defiance. 'I'm much better with horses, this is true.'

She'd made him smile—and given the morning he'd had this was quite an accomplishment. 'Thank you.'

'For what? Giving bad advice?' She waved him away. 'Go. Go make my horse look good.'

The Angelique of his youth had been naïve, too trusting and wholly ignorant of the life he was being trained to. This one was jaded, politically aware and brutally honest—with herself as well as him. She was magnificent. 'I will.'

She nodded, once. 'Might make you look good too.'

* * *

Angelique made a point of watching every game in which Cordova horses played. She didn't trust second-hand accounts of the play and considered her presence a business requirement rather than a pleasure. Some games were excruciating to watch, like the one yesterday, but this game was different. Competitive, professional, sportsmanlike and thrilling.

Valentine, infertile King of Thallasia, rode as if he'd ridden her mare for years. Strong. Confident. Devastatingly effective. Merciless against his opposition, and beneath it all the skill to keep his mount safe and engaged, rested when the opportunity arose and all too willing when riding for goal. Even Lucia clapped his latest goal, appreciation for his skill outweighing years of dislike.

'You're clapping him,' Angelique observed with outright astonishment.

'I can't help it. Did you see that goal? He rides like you.'

'You mean he rides like he has something to prove?' She was enjoying the way her favourite mare shone beneath his guidance. No one could deny Valentine's expertise, his skill, his fairness. He looked *good* out there. Not sick or struggling or anything less than overwhelmingly *virile*. 'He thinks I pity him.'

'You have to admit it's quite a blow for a king to be sterile. If it's true.'

'It's true. I just asked him.'

Lucia grimaced. 'Poor man.'

'He's not poor! Or suddenly incompetent or incapable of ruling his country. Look at him!'

'I'm looking.' The slightest hint of indulgence had crept into Lucia's voice. 'Great seat, strong legs, *very* nice goal. Your "tough love" approach seems to be working for him. We should clap again.'

'He infuriates me.' In all fairness, he was playing exceptionally well. 'I don't know what to do with him.'

Lucia turned her attention from the polo match to Angelique. 'Last night you wanted nothing to do with him.'

And today it was different.

'You still want him. That's just fact.' Lucia didn't wait for any comment. 'And now he's no longer obliged to marry a Thallasian noblewoman and provide children for his throne you think you can have him? Is that what you think?'

'I—' She knew it was crazy and unhealthy and wrong, but, 'Yes.'

'What about children?' Her sister never had been one to mince words, and these ones were designed to provoke, to make her think. Maybe even to make her hurt.

Because she did hurt at the thought of missing out on being part of a traditional family one day. Did she really want to forgo the chance to hold her son or daughter in her arms, to love beyond measure and watch her children grow? And for what? A man who might never even acknowledge a relationship with her, let alone her sacrifice?

And yet...

If she came to love Valentine, truly love him, and he loved and valued her too, and children weren't for him... 'What about them?'

CHAPTER FIVE

KING VALENTINE OF THALLASIA played four consecutive chukkas, rode two more of her horses, and then the mare Armonía again at the last, and secured his team six goals and the competition win. It had been a masterful performance and everyone knew it. He weathered Theo's ribbing and the congratulations of his teammates with a shrug and a faintly pleased grin. Arrogance personified, she might have once said. Right up until he caught her eye and let the briefest glimpse of vulnerability show in his flashing black eyes.

Have I pleased you? Did I ride well?

And then the bright flare of relief when she responded by inclining her head in a wordless gesture of approval.

And then it was time for her to take the mare and for him to disappear, only he somehow stayed behind when the others moved on.

'You do realise everyone's watching us,' she murmured.

'I'm aware.'

'But you don't care? Still in self-destruct mode, then? Planning on going out with a bang?'

'I'll give you four million euros for the mare,' he countered, at which point Angelique all but tripped over her own feet. At best, the mare would fetch eight hundred thousand euros and that was assuming the buyer had no common sense and money to burn. An offer of four million was ridiculous.

'How much?'

'Four million euros. But there's a catch.'

'And I can't wait to hear it, but you should probably cool down before you make any rash offers.' Valentine was fresh off the field and flush with the endorphins that came with riding an animal that had catered to his every whim. It wouldn't be fair to take advantage of him.

Unfair, yet still altogether tempting.

She took the mare's reins and let Valentine fall into step beside her as they walked along the sidelines to cool the horse down.

'Four million for the mare and the catch is I want one month of your time. One month, and you'll live in my palace, rejuvenate Thallasia's royal horse-breeding programme and breakfast with me daily.'

'I'm not a breakfast person.' She tossed her head and glared at an over-curious group of spectators heading towards them. 'Besides, the Cordovas no longer sell horses to Thallasia.'

'So I've noticed,' he drawled. 'And I want that embargo lifted.'

'Then you need to speak with my father.'

'And I will. With your permission.' He seemed intent on walking them far from the spectator crowd. 'Did I mention the part about you coming to Thallasia and using your horse-breeding expertise for my benefit?'

'Isn't Alessandro still with you?' She knew for a fact he was. Over the years the old horseman had stayed in regular contact with her father about the progress of the foals she'd left behind.

'He is, and I'm sure he'd appreciate your input.'

In her experience, men who considered themselves experts in their field rarely appreciated any input. And then there was the whole 'I told you so' element of meeting the old horsemaster again after so thoroughly ignoring his advice to stay away from Valentine all those years ago. She still felt a healthy dose of shame for the way she'd jeopardised the man's career, and time hadn't lessened it. 'The point *being* that if Alessandro wants advice about the Cordova bloodlines in his care, all he has to do is pick up the phone and call my father.' Just because her father would sell no more horses to Valentine, didn't mean he wasn't still fully invested in the care of the horses he'd already parted with. 'You don't need me staying under your roof for that.'

'Then consider this offer my way of saying I want

to see you again, and, given that I can't come to you, I'm quite prepared to pay you to come to me.'

'You want a mistress. For a month.' Was that his goal?

'No.'

Then she didn't understand. The horse shifted restlessly beneath her hand. Time to turn around and make their way back to the stables.

'Is it so hard to believe that I want to get to know you all over again, slowly and with no commitment on either side beyond a certain willingness to see where it leads?' His eyes were guarded, his stride relaxed. Jodhpurs did amazing things to his thighs and the thin sheen of sweat on his forearms brought corded muscles and veins into strong relief. He set her senses aflame just as easily today as he had last night, there was no denying it. Always had. Probably always would. And if anyone had made her feel *half* the attraction she felt for him, she might not have been nearly so willing to listen to his offer, but no one ever had.

'You know my limitations,' he muttered. 'No children, no need to marry. That's me. And if you're not interested, say so now and that will be the end of it.'

They kept walking. Angelique tried to find her voice, her pride, something to shake her from her stupor, but silence ruled. Silence and a world of what if.

'Offer for the horse, by all means,' she said finally. 'My father might indulge you if you're persuasive enough. I couldn't say.' She smiled lopsidedly. 'Safe to say I find you attractive. That hasn't changed. But I don't want some made-up job that takes me away from my real work, and I won't put my life on hold for you. What I *am* prepared to do is try and find a way to make our lives intersect more.'

'Angelique, if you're expecting me to travel, the planning and security alone—'

'Stop. Hear me out.' She knew who he was. She didn't expect miracles. 'My family has been looking to buy or lease horse-training facilities in Liesendaach. We've not looked towards Thallasia, but maybe we could. And then we could see to unfinished business. Slake our thirst, and, when that's done, I'll still have a career I love and a fulfilling life to be going on with that doesn't include you. You do not monopolise my time. When it comes to your royal duties, you're on your own. And when this…' she gestured between them '…this unfinished sexual attraction between us has run its course we finish it.'

'Just like that?'

'No, not just like that.' She could see the split now and it would be messy and altogether too public and everyone would say I told you so, and she would be that woman—the one who kept coming back for more punishment and humiliation at the hands of a man who did not deserve her love. 'I have one more demand of you and it's to do with what happens once our time has run its course.'

'You seem so very sure it will.'

'Aren't you?' How could he possibly think otherwise? 'I know my reputation probably can't get any worse, but when we walk away, I want your respect. If someone I don't even know condemns me in public so be it, but you—you who know me and are about to know my friends and family—I want your word that you won't badmouth me to them. You do what you failed to do before, and that's stand up for my honour and my right to enter and exit a relationship with dignity, and without being called a conniving whore.'

He looked shell-shocked. Maybe because her words had come from a place of such deep hurt and she'd spoken them openly.

Maybe she fully expected him to turn and walk away and relieve her of the burden of willingly entering into such a foolish agreement with him. But he didn't go, and she couldn't breathe.

'I'm sorry.' She barely heard his raspy words. 'I owe you an apology, not just for the fallout and loss of reputation you endured, but for compromising you in the first place. I should have known better. But I'm not that man any more and I will never allow anyone to speak ill of you in my presence. You have my word.'

An apology. Years too late and just as anguished and heartfelt as she could have ever imagined.

She had no idea what to say next. 'How much land do you need?' Fortunately for her, he turned to more practical matters.

'Three to five hundred acres, plus stables for at least thirty horses, and a house for me to live in.'

'What kind of house?'

'Nothing fancy.'

'What kind of price?' he asked.

'Depends on the place. Leasing's also an option. I can't imagine you wanting me within reach for ever.'

'You've made it very clear you don't want to be within reach for ever.' He gave her a long, level look. 'I'll see if I hold any land suitable for your needs.'

'You do that.' She let the silence envelop them, rich with possibilities. 'So we're really going to do this? You and me?'

'Looks like.'

'We're both mad. You know this, right?'

His laughter rang out, and, oh, how she'd missed it. 'I know this.' He smiled, warm and wide, and she'd missed that too. 'Yes.'

CHAPTER SIX

THE WEEKS THAT followed were, without doubt, some of the most brutal Valentine had ever experienced, and that included his years in the military and the dark months surrounding his father's demise. Secure the crown. Stabilise the country. Vala and his advisors, neighbouring kings included, had persuaded him to stay on as monarch and bring the issue of heirs to the throne to the forefront of national conversation. His publicity team had worked triple time trying to secure positive press for the crown as Thallasia rumbled and roiled its way around to recognising that his twin sister—younger by a matter of mere minutes—was now permanently first in line to the throne, and that his niece Juliana was the next generation's heir apparent.

As to the matter of his broken engagement, speculation was rife as to whether he would ever marry now that heirs were no longer part of the deal. The headlines spun the stories and he lost track of the reactions the press bestowed on him. Everything from

Suicidal to *Free and Easy* got a run, never mind that he was neither. He'd been linked to no fewer than nine different women this past week alone—and it didn't seem to matter that he hadn't seen three of them in over a decade. His media team had deemed it prudent to create a standard letter of apology for him to dispense as needed. Four supposed illegitimate heirs had been revealed by tabloid journalists. All had been investigated and debunked, but still they took their toll on the nation's faith in his leadership.

Today's article was a recap of his history with Angelique, and a list of her accomplishments since then. Many of those accomplishments were on the sordid side. A list of men she'd been associated with—Theo included. Her longstanding on and off relationship with Benedict—which Valentine now knew had been nothing more than a cover for Benedict hooking up with her brother. Didn't stop the press from salivating over pictures of her and Benedict dancing on some outdoor nightclub stage. Or speculating on the sloppy, intimate smile Benedict had been sending someone over her shoulder. They'd been indulging in a wild threesome that night, according to the article. Just another regular night out for Angelique.

The recap then went on to discuss a night out in Mallorca that had ended with several arrests, Angelique's included—although she'd later been cleared of all charges. A stint on an All-Stars Polo team, complete with luxury watch ambassadorship deal. The accompanying picture was a beauty. Angelique in riding gear, with a fierce expression, a thoroughbred horse beside her and an expensive timepiece on her wrist. It was a smouldering, sexy, challenging approach, guaranteed to fire the blood and make a man want all those expensive things that lay just out of ordinary reach. The promise being that if you were rich enough, remarkable enough, lucky enough, you too might be able to possess such power, precision and beauty.

She seemed to be wanted and vilified in the same breath, for the same reasons. He knew full well that the press was going to make a meal out of her when he entered the picture again. Kinder all round to leave her alone, but he simply couldn't do it. Just like all those years ago when he hadn't been able to stay away, no matter how dire the warning.

He had to believe that things were different this time. That change happened from the top down and that this time he could protect her from those who would seek to destroy her simply because they could.

To have her exit a relationship with him more beaten up than when she went into it was unthinkable.

Respect had to start from the top.

She had to enter his domain cloaked in as much honour and respect for her needs as he could give her.

It took him two days to identify a duchy and

manor house suitable for Angelique's needs. But it took him another two weeks to set up a meeting with Angelique's father at the family estate in Spain, and that meant travel and security arrangements and no small expense, and having to explain his actions to his sister, who was already irritated by her new-found celebrity. She'd gone from being happy spare to scrutinised heir, and she was up to the task, no question. He'd never doubted it.

Didn't mean she had to like it.

'I'm filling in for you at the most important royal banquet of the year because you're going where?' His sister's voice was dangerously mild and completely at odds with the hard glint in her eyes.

'Spain, to meet with the Cordova patriarch and offer him the use of a duchy.'

'You see, that's what I thought you said. At which point I immediately thought I must be mistaken. Is this about a horse?'

'No. It's about apologising to the father of the woman I wronged many years ago.'

'Valentine. Dearest.' Her sister sat back in the library chair she'd commandeered, elbows on the arm rests and her fingers steepled in front of her. She wore a simple blue shift with silver trim, diamonds at her ears and on her wrist, and her hair had been woven in a complex weave once favoured by the likes of Grace Kelly. No one who looked hard enough would ever doubt the razor-sharp ability to read people that lurked beneath her surface beauty.

'Trust me when I say you've wronged more than one woman in your lifetime and dare I suggest you'll do so again before you're dead? You start giving spare duchies to every one of them, we're going to run out of land.'

Okay, so perhaps he did have a few small reparations to make but who didn't? He'd get to them.

'I'm not bestowing the duchy. I'm offering to let the Cordova family company lease it for a modest sum in return for their collaboration when it comes to the breeding programme for Thallasia's royal horses. We're falling behind in the prize horse stakes. I don't like falling behind.'

'Horses.' His sister saw straight through that particular excuse.

'The Cordovas do specialise in horses, yes.'

'But it's not really about horses, is it? This is about Angelique.'

'She does factor into the calculation, yes.'

'God help us, not again.'

'Why not?' If Vala wanted an argument, he'd give her one. 'It's not as if she'll ever be the future mother of my children.'

'Do you *know* how insulting you're being?'

When would he learn not to lead with that argument when there was no winning with it? 'And by that, I mean she won't be subject to the kind of scrutiny any wife of mine would receive. If I were to take up with Angelique in an unofficial capacity, no labels required, surely she would escape that dubious honour?'

'Don't be so sure.'

'Or I could keep any relationship with her low-key and therefore of little interest to others.'

'Because that worked so well for you last time you tried it,' his sister snapped, standing up and putting her hands on her hips. How anyone could spend time with her these days and think her a lightweight with no real authority or inclination to wield it was beyond him. She was the mother of three young children, including four-year-old twins. She'd been wielding authority effectively for years. Over them. Over her husband. And all too often now, over him. 'Honestly, Valentine, don't you ever learn? If you want to be with Angelique, at least do her and everyone else the service of publicly and proudly admitting it.'

He could do that. 'All right. This is me, owning my desire. I want Angelique in my bed and in my life and, the way I see it, apologising to her family for my sins against her and them is the first step towards me getting what I want. I'm trying to make amends. I don't need your permission.'

His sister scowled. 'Way to get me onside.'

'I do want you onside. Also at my side, ready to step up and rule if need be.'

His sister winced, her discomfort obvious. 'Don't leave me holding the crown, Val. I won't do it justice. The polls want you to stay on as King.' And hadn't that been a pleasant surprise, in amongst the daily headlines? 'I know you were thinking about other options.'

'I made a deal with myself,' he admitted gruffly. 'Stay and serve and in return I get to try and carve out a personal life that pleases me.'

'Has your heart really stayed true to the little stable girl all these years?'

He shrugged, uncomfortable with the question. 'What does it matter? That girl no longer exists. But the woman she became is almost within reach, and I want to get to know her better. I'm not going to compromise her. This time I can protect her and I intend to.'

'All right. Your happiness is important to me, never doubt it.' His sister's voice was no longer deceptively light and airy. Instead, it weighed heavy with comfort and understanding. 'Let's bring her within reach.'

It was easy to be impressed by the Cordova family estate in the northernmost reaches of Spain. The lush green pastures and mountain backdrop catered beautifully to the raising of horses. Mile upon mile of immaculate wooden fencing, laneways and shelters crisscrossed the hillsides and valleys. Stables made of tile and stone dotted the landscape, and the main house was set low and wide against a natural escarpment that allowed for views that seemed to stretch on for ever. An aura of quiet wealth, con-

tentment, and sensitive stewardship stirred the air
here. A maze of stone-walled gardens surrounded
the main house and pushed visitors towards a
U-shaped entrance driveway.

Eduardo Cordova was there to meet him as he
got out of the car. Valentine's security detail had
preceded him by minutes and were now spread like
points of the compass, barely visible but there all the
same. The Cordova patriarch regarded him thought-
fully, seemingly untroubled by the cavalcade. Given
the list of royalty and billionaire families he regularly sold horses to, he was probably used to it.

'Señor Cordova.' Valentine held out his hand,
not wanting or waiting for awkwardness to arrive.
'Thank you for agreeing to see me.' He counted it a
win when the other man nodded and shook his out-
stretched hand before gesturing towards an archway
to the left of the large main doors.

'My office. This is not my family's first encounter
with those who travel with bodyguards. Your people have assured me our meeting place meets their
needs. They can protect you from there and sight
you as well.' The archway led to a modest outdoor
area with a central tree laden with lemons, a pond
full of water plants, ample outdoor seating, and access to the house via glass doors that opened up one
wall of a long library room almost completely. Two
of Valentine's guards were already in residence, one
in the courtyard, another just inside a closed door
that led further inside the house. 'Come.'

The older man headed towards a cluster of low tables and tan leather club chairs. One of the tables had been set with refreshments for two. 'Please, take a seat. Tell me, do kings still use poison tasters?'

Valentine took a seat that afforded him a view of the courtyard and the interior door both. 'Not that I know of.'

Angelique's father smiled and sat opposite. 'Coffee?'

'Please.' He watched as the other man poured.

'I have to say, I'm puzzled as to why you're here.' The older man settled back into his chair and made no move towards the fragrant brew he'd just served. 'I've already told you that the mare you want is not for sale.'

'And yet you've sold horses out from beneath your daughter before.'

'Not ones of this calibre. You're wasting your time if that's all you came for.'

'That's not all I came for.'

The old man's gaze didn't leave his face. 'I don't read minds.'

No one said making this apology was going to be easy. 'I wish to extend my sincere apology for the treatment I afforded your daughter, and by extension your family, all those years ago. I was young, foolish and arrogant and I regret my part in your family's fall from grace.'

'And there it is. The arrogance of kings,' the other

man murmured. 'My family did not fall from grace. We merely stopped having anything to do with you.'

'My loss, certainly. To that end, I wish to offer Angelique, and by extension your family business, leasehold access to a modest duchy situated on the Thallasia-Liesendaach border. It consists of a manor house, the surrounding grazing land and forests and several smaller dwellings. A gatehouse, a hunting lodge, a groundskeeper's cottage. It has a manager, a gardener and a housekeeper—all paid for by the income from the estate. Some of the land is currently used for cropping, some of it for grazing. All of it perfect for horses. There is no duke or duchess—the title has been rotated out of use and remains with the crown. There are no plans to resurrect it.'

'And what makes you think we could ever afford a lease on such an estate?'

'A hundred thousand Euros per annum and Cordova consultancy services when it comes to re-invigorating the bloodlines of the royal horses of Thallasia says you probably can.' It was barely enough to cover the cost of the people already in place and who would stay in place to serve Angelique.

'And what's in it for you?'

'A chance to get to know Angelique on her terms. Nothing more, nothing less.'

'Not exactly a salesman, are you?'

'No, I'm a king.'

'You realise that my blessing is not all you need

for your endeavour to succeed? You need my daughter's agreement as well.'

'I already have it.'

'Oh, *do* you?'

'More or less.' Possibly less.

The older man finally picked up his coffee and set it to his lips. Weathered, lean and wiry, he somehow managed to project a far bigger presence than his small stature afforded him. 'So, assuming you do manage to persuade my daughter within reach, what then? Do you intend to marry her?'

'No.'

'And children are not for you either, so I'm given to understand.'

'True.'

'You don't have much to offer her, do you?'

Valentine leaned towards his coffee cup, taking his time to add two cubes of sugar and stir well before lifting the fragrant brew to his lips. He had no arguments to counter the other man's observations. He knew Angelique deserved more and yet here he was. 'I have the arrogance of kings. That and the sure belief that if your daughter had wanted marriage to a man who loved her and children to complete that pretty picture, she would have had that by now.'

'She's young. She can still have all that.'

Although not if she takes up with you.

Those words sat there between them, unspoken but present. 'True. But not with me. She knows that.'

The coffee was good. Best he'd ever tasted. Perhaps it was the pure mountain air and lack of bull. The fact that Angelique's father was giving him no quarter at all.

'My children have a tendency to love as they will,' the older man said at last. 'My son loves a man. Damn near broke my heart but here I am, heart-whole and thriving and my son is the happiest I've ever seen him. He loves without reservation and is loved just as much in return, and I am content. Love is love, isn't that the phrase?' He nodded to himself. 'If my daughter decides she loves you, with all the complexities involved, do you have the heart to love her in return?'

Not for a moment did he hesitate, and it wasn't just the arrogance of kings. 'I will cut out my heart before I hurt her again.'

Three weeks later, Angelique and thirty-six of the Cordova family's finest horses moved into Valentine's spare estate. Valentine had made his offer the day after he'd visited her father, and what they had spoken of neither would say, but her father had backed her decision to take on the lease, and the property really was perfect for their needs. Less travel for the polo ponies. Beautiful facilities. She could even repurpose part of the huge expanse of manicured lawn as a polo field, although the gardener would likely need resuscitating.

She'd searched her heart and decided to take a

chance on this new chapter in her life. No marriage or babies on her horizon but an eventful and privileged future no less. She'd said yes to the lease. Yes to whatever might eventuate between her and Valentine. Yes to the crazy bad portrayal of her in the press, just as soon as they got wind of the transaction between the Thallasian monarchy and the Cordova horsemasters. Just yes.

Her whole family descended on the day she moved in. Her brother, Carlos, and Benedict, Luciana, and her parents. Even Queen Consort Moriana, along with Moriana's favourite lady-in-waiting and one extremely good-looking guardsman of Liesendaach, had snuck in to help Angelique take possession. Never had Angelique imagined the immaculately put-together Moriana tucking into three different kinds of paella, plus salads, and then plain old *natillas*—or custard—for dessert, elbow to elbow with Angelique's family and her employees. Never underestimate the woman, that was the take home.

Angelique had yet to understand why Moriana was even there.

'But this is wonderful.' Moriana sighed her contentment. 'Theo will be so sad to have missed this.'

'The slumming?' Angelique teased, and waited to see how the other woman would take it.

'Hardly.' Moriana waved her hand towards the rest of the hall with its fourteen bedrooms and umpteen sitting rooms and dining areas. 'The freedom to be with you all and not be on our best royal behaviour. I dripped paella on my napkin. I have opened up rooms for airing. Directed a hay truck down to the stables.'

'Raided Valentine's wine cellar,' murmured Benedict with a benevolent smile.

'You suggested it,' Angelique reminded him dryly. 'And I swear, you will be replacing it, because I'm damn sure I haven't a hope of buying any of these bottles again. This one's twenty years old and comes from a monastery I've never heard of.'

'And where *is* Valentine this weekend?' Moriana asked. 'I half expected him to put in an appearance.'

She wasn't the only one. 'I did invite him.' Angelique held up her hands in all innocence. 'Not for a meal, mind, but he knew we were coming in this weekend and that we'd all be here. I told him he was free to drop in any time. Not that kings drop in.'

'They don't?' said a voice from the doorway, and there stood Valentine in what for him counted as casual clothes. Dark trousers, perfectly pressed. A dove-grey business shirt, rolled to the sleeves and with the top buttons undone. No security detail in sight, although presumably they were around somewhere. 'I did knock. And when no one came to the door, I followed the noise.'

'Valentine!' Moriana was the only one there who was anywhere near his equal in rank, and when she stood immediately, everyone else began to, whether they'd finished their meal or not.

'Don't.' He held up his hand for everyone to stop. 'Please. Finish your meals. I've come at an inconvenient time.'

'Or you could pull up a chair and have some paella and drink some of your wine,' Angelique offered, and meant every word of it. 'What happens at Raven Hall stays at Raven Hall. It's the new rule.'

She could see him assessing everyone in the room. Her parents, Luciana, Carlos and Benedict, Moriana and her retinue. 'No Theo?' he murmured, and Moriana waved a dismissive hand.

'His loss.'

Carlos dragged a chair across and placed it between himself and their father. Lucia snorted inelegantly and Angelique bit back a smile. Had the very fine-looking King of Thallasia ever been subjected to a Spanish family's intimidation tactics? She doubted it, even as she rose to get him a glass for the wine and a plate and utensils for the food on the table. 'It's serve yourself, although Carlos might be persuaded to fill your glass. It's yours, by the way, the wine.'

'That was my doing.' Benedict came clean, and Angelique laughed outright.

'What's this I hear? Is that your conscience speaking?'

'Only because I owe you.'

'So very much,' Lucia murmured.

And Carlos raised his glass and said, 'I'll drink to that,' so everyone did and it became a toast and then conversation resumed between Moriana and Lucia, between Benedict and her mother, between Carlos and her father as they talked straight through Valentine, who looked at his empty plate and then at her and then picked up a serving spoon and dug into her mother's monster pan of seafood paella.

'Good choice,' said Carlos, and Valentine nodded and glanced Angelique's way again.

'So I hear.'

'Nice place you have here,' said her father.

'Yes.'

'Rent it out often?' asked Benedict, full of barbs and doublespeak, and Angelique aimed a well-deserved kick at him beneath the table. 'Ouch! You kicked me.'

'Did I hit anything important?' Own your actions, an old lesson learned well. She smiled sweetly, and winked at Valentine, the poor outnumbered soul.

Who was he when he wasn't being a king? She truly didn't know.

It was hard to say if even *he* knew, but he was no stranger to social situations and general awkwardness, that much was clear as he picked food as a topic and drew her parents into a conversation about their favourite meals and memories, and places too, until soon everyone was joining in, and it was fun to simply sit and watch him watching them.

After dinner Carlos, Benedict and her father drew him away to one of the sitting rooms while she and Lucia stayed back and helped clear the table.

Moriana stayed too, a queen doing dishes, and she laughed and said she had the better of the deal, so Lucia opened another bottle of wine for them all.

'He wants you,' Moriana said to Angelique, and no one needed to put a name to those words.

'I know.'

'Are you going to let him have you?'

'I think so. I don't need marriage. I'm not interested in status. I don't care that he can't give me children. And if he wants to make waves and annoy those in his court who sought to bring him down, I'm just the woman to help him make a statement.'

'True,' said Moriana. 'I like it.'

'I don't.' Lucia pointed a clean wooden spoon in Angelique's direction. 'That's ninety per cent bravado talking, and ten per cent delusion. You're going to fall for him all over again and there'll be so many pieces to pick up at the end that we won't be able to find them all.'

'Lucia's a bit of a pessimist,' her mother explained to Moriana, and then it was on.

'Me? *Me* the pessimist?' This from Lucia and she had a wooden spoon in her hand and Angelique started running. Around the table and through the doorway and straight into the arms of the man they'd all been talking about. Thankfully, he was alone.

'And stay out!' Luciana's voice followed them from the doorway, as Angelique disengaged her elbow from his solar plexus and her cheek from his chest.

'Sisterly love?' he asked, and she could feel the

deep rumble of his voice through his chest, because her hand was still on it, and she had two choices. She could either snatch her hand back and step away or she could stay right where she was and start smoothing him out. She chose the latter.

If his lazy grin was anything to go by, it was the right choice. 'I left your men in the study with my liquor. Let me know when you need more cellar supplies and I'll have it restocked. Especially if you take to entertaining Liesendaach royalty on a regular basis. Will your family be here often?'

'No, they're only here to help me move in. They have their own lives.'

'But you do seem close.'

'They're my strength.' They'd had their spats, but they'd also had to close ranks over and over again through the years. First when Angelique had run afoul of the Thallasian monarchy, and again when Carlos took up with Benedict.

'Should I expect a chaperone every time I visit?'

'Hardly.' Though Lucia would probably find it fun to watch his frustration grow. 'My family will remain silent if you wish for any association between you and me to remain a secret. You only have to look to my brother's relationship with Benedict to see that they can. That's been going on for the last seven, no, eight years.'

His lips tightened. 'With you as the beard.'

She shrugged, because basically yes. 'Sometimes

Lucia pretending to be me, but yes. The fact is, my family is discreet.'

'What if I don't want to hide my relationship with you? Are you interested at all in being seen with me in public?'

'To step into the limelight with you all over again and have your country's gutter press tear into me like a pack of mountain wolves? Why not?' She would be playing to type, after all. 'It's my specialty. Part of my appeal. The unsuitable woman, no?'

'No.'

Her steps faltered and she slid him a sideways glance. The hallway sconces threw his features into stark relief. Beauty and shadows, always the shadows with him. 'You're not intending to use my wanton reputation to shore up your poor beleaguered masculinity?'

'No.'

'Oh.' Now she was just plain confused.

'Let's just say that while I don't want to hide my interest in you, nor do I intend to throw you to the wolves. I'd rather protect you. The way I never did before.'

She frowned.

'The national art gallery is opening a new exhibition area on Thursday and I'm saying a few words and staying on for a couple of hours afterwards. I'd like you to accompany me. It will draw comment, of that I have no doubt. Your leasing of this place may be unearthed. But the sooner I indicate my official interest in you and bring the palace's media machine on board, the better for you. I have no intention of treating you like a dirty secret. Not this time. Never again. Let's aim to do this right.'

His sincerity was her undoing. They could never rewrite the past, but the future looked promising.

'We good?' he asked.

'Get your people to send me a brief—and by that I mean what you'll be wearing to the gallery opening, what others will be wearing, and who the main dignitaries are. It's the kind of brief Moriana makes up for Carlos and Benedict all the time. Works a treat.'

'That woman…' He shook his head.

'Inspiring, isn't she? You'd best say goodbye to her and the others in the kitchen if you're taking your leave. Of course, you could always stay. No one has taken possession of the master bedroom yet. It's free.'

'Why did no one take the master?'

'Could have something to do with the bear rug in front of the hearth and the stuffed leopard looking down from the ceiling joists. And then there's the monkeys.'

'Monkeys?' he repeated.

'You've never stayed here before, have you?'

'No. Can't say I'm familiar with the layout of the place beyond what's on a set of plans back at the palace.'

The perils of heading a monarchy. And, boy, was he in for a treat. 'Let me give you the tour.'

CHAPTER SEVEN

THERE WAS SOMETHING surreal about having Angelique give him a tour of a manor house he owned.
He'd come to visit her on a whim, not intending to
pursue her before she'd even settled in, but his desire to see her again had overridden common sense.
She was nearby and he'd sped through all his work
for the day and was at a loose end. In his imagination she had been alone and half expecting him. A
diaphanous nightgown and a sultry smile had fea-
tured heavily in his daydream. She'd been wearing
them when she opened the door to him…

His libido had clearly not died along with his
ability to procreate.

Nor, apparently, had his imagination.

In reality, he'd knocked on the huge manor house
doors and when no one had responded he'd gone
round the back and, led by the noise, had let himself into the wet room and followed the scent of food
through to the kitchen door. He'd somehow found
himself sitting down to what amounted to a Cordova

family dinner. Shedding his kingly persona bit by bit as the evening wore on, watching Moriana let her hair down with no little astonishment, enjoying Benedict's razor-sharp tongue and Carlos' calming presence in a room full of volatile people. Luciana and Angelique so *different* from one another underneath their near identical features. The Cordova matriarch so beloved by them all, and Eduardo Cordova presiding proudly at the head of the table. A generous, gregarious man, with a steady hand on the reins of his family and an air of unwavering love and support.

For Valentine, whose family life had never been nurturing, it was like stepping into a whole new world.

After dinner, he'd made sure the drawing room had been stocked with the best the cellar could provide and had then made up some flimsy excuse to seek out Angelique. Fortunately, he'd found her alone, and now she was giving him the tour, her face flushed and her saunter relaxed. Her jeans, high boots and floral cotton top with a drawstring loose around her neck suited the informality of the evening and showcased her generous curves. He definitely had a thing for boots, he decided, and mentally shredded the diaphanous nightgown.

Only to have his brain helpfully replace it with an image of Angelique wearing boots and lacy pink lingerie with little bows.

The manor house had not been made for comfort or for nesting. Ceilings soared, bedrooms were huge and the dining rooms gilded with thick golden drapes of crushed velvet. Stone lined the floors, a mixture of grey and mossy green slate. The floor rugs were threadbare and the furniture heavy hand-carved dark wood. The entire manor had a faded, medieval air about it.

And then came the master bedroom—a circus from start to finish, what with the leopard prints and the zebra stripes and the ruby-red drapes and various stuffed animals. The leopard prowling the ceiling beams, as promised. A stuffed monkey hanging from the ceiling light. 'Moriana saw this?' he asked.

'Sure did. She said you win on the mad décor front, although her brother has a round room for courtesans that takes some beating. It has a trapeze.' She eyed the manacles bolted to a nearby wall. 'I didn't ask if it had restraints. Who used to live here?'

'A duke, a hundred years ago. Change whatever you want. There's likely an attic full of spare furniture somewhere.'

'There is, and we've already raided it. I only intend to occupy half a dozen rooms at most, and we spent the weekend making them comfortable. And the horse facilities are everything we could ask for and more. We're happy with the move and so we should be.' Her eyes drifted towards the ceiling and another stuffed monkey occupying a beam. 'Monkeys included. Plus I've had a few more minutes to think about being your date for the art gallery open-

ing, and I'm happy with that too. I'm ready for you.'
The look she sent him was pure smoulder.

'So if I was to kiss you right now, before I take
my leave, that would be an acceptable end to the
evening?'

'Yes.'

He'd kissed her before, all those years ago. He
thought he remembered her passion and sweet-
ness but it was nothing compared to what he tasted
now. He let himself sink, undone, overwhelmed. He
wanted nothing more than to pull her down onto
the bed and take all the time in the world to discover her all over again. But there were monkeys
overhead, and her family just down the hall and he
wouldn't put it past any of them to go looking for
her. He could wait. He'd waited this long, after all.
They had time.

'Come back here after the gallery opening,' she
murmured and drew him down for another kiss.
'Can that be arranged beforehand?'

'Presumptuous.'

'Yes, I am. I know enough about kings to know
that spontaneity is hard to come by. So let's plan.
Or am I moving too fast for you?'

Oh, challenge accepted. 'Your room. Now.'

He'd never seen her move so swiftly in the other
direction. 'With my parents in the house? Never.'

It felt so good to laugh and pretend to be that care-
free boy again—the one who had played and loved

without reservation. Fearless, in a way he'd never been since. 'I'll see myself out, shall I?'

'I can walk you to the door.' She looked around. 'If I can find it.'

They found it together. His security team filtered in from their positions and she clocked them all and nodded but said nothing. 'Thank you for the meal,' he offered.

'What did you think of the paella?'

It wasn't just the food. It was the atmosphere around the table that made the meal so memorable, the warmth and wit and welcome extended to him. 'I've never tasted better.'

CHAPTER EIGHT

FOUR DAYS LATER, Valentine stood on the steps of the art gallery and watched Angelique alight from the vehicle he'd sent to collect her. He'd worked long hours all week so he could take tomorrow morning off, and he had every intention of enjoying himself this evening. If Angelique's presence at his side caused a stir, so be it. The people of Thallasia would simply have to get used to it.

She wore scarlet—of course she did, and her shoulders were bare and her hair had been artfully piled on top of her head and held in place by pins tipped with pearls to match the three-strand pearl choker at her neck. That choker had a leash on it—he had no idea what else to call it—that dangled down her back to rest just above the curve of her utterly perfect rear. He could pick it up and reel her in and his hand itched to take hold of it.

She saw him moments later and put her arms out and twirled. 'Will I do?'

'What exactly are you aiming for?'

'Well, the exhibition's called *The Downfall of Man*—it's an inspired first-date choice, by the way. I thought I'd stick to theme.'

'Good job.'

'Although there's really only one man whose downfall I wish to be associated with, and that's yours.'

'Still with the revenge theme.'

Her megawatt smile almost blinded him. 'That's what they'll say, and I do aim to please.'

He held out his arm for her to take, and felt a jolt of possessive satisfaction when her slender hand covered his arm. 'You certainly do. Do you need a powder room before we're announced?'

'Wouldn't hurt.'

'Are you nervous?' She didn't look it.

'I'd be mad not to be. But there's a difference between nervous and ready, and I'm ready.'

They caused a stir on entry to the exhibition as he had known they would, and she bore it all with a flair for mischief that shouldn't have surprised him as much as it did. She genuinely enjoyed the exhibition, it seemed, and stayed attentive during the speeches. She didn't simper, cling, or go out of her way to impress. At one point she winked at him and almost derailed his speech.

The ease with which she navigated his world surprised him, though perhaps it shouldn't have. They'd spent years travelling in similar circles, overlapping, rarely meeting.

His sister was in attendance and made a point of joining Angelique to view several of the paintings together. Enough to imply approval of his choice of guest for the evening. He nodded his thanks and she raised a brow and excused herself from Angelique's side and began to work the room in earnest—backing up the efforts he'd already put in. Not just the spare to be sidelined, she'd stepped up to present a united front alongside him and begun to let people glimpse the formidable intellect beneath the looks she'd always relied on to impress them.

Angelique welcomed him with a smile as he held out his arm for her to take and moved them on to the next picture.

'Kind of your sister to publicly endorse me,' she murmured. 'Did you put her up to it?'

'No. She likes that I'm falling in favour and that her power is rising. I'm giving her more responsibility, and for all that she may not have wanted it, she wields it beautifully. Makes it easier for me to move over.'

'You're still considering abdication?'

'Not any more. No. But it doesn't hurt people to see King Valentine with his twin at his side. They're getting two for the price of one. They should be pleased. Anyone give you trouble here this evening?'

'With you here watching them, and me, like a hawk? Who would dare?'

'Oh, I think you'll find that the papers tomorrow will dare.'

She shrugged dismissively. 'Don't expect me to care. My family is the foundation on which I stand, and they know who I am.' She looked so beautiful with her flashing black eyes and the scarlet draping her curves. 'I'm more worried about the fallout you'll face.'

'It can hardly be worse than being rendered less than a man and a failure as a king for being unable to provide an heir. "You had one job…"' he began, and she laughed, because, seriously, who knew he could do voices?

But it wasn't just the voices. He was beginning to accept his new limits and move forward, and she respected him for that.

And wanted to undress him very soon.

It wasn't a normal date, by any means, and when it ended and his driver took them to her place, which was technically his place, his security detail checking through the house put an end to all thoughts of ravishing him the moment they stepped through the doors. Still, there was a certain satisfaction in seeing him methodically unwind after being on show for the evening. They started in the study her visitors seemed to favour—the one with the deep library chairs and the side bar stuffed full of spirits and cut-glass crystal. She watched as he removed his jacket and slung it over the back of a chair before loosening his tie and then removing his cufflinks one by one before making a beeline for the drinks.

He'd been offered champagne on arrival at the

gallery and had taken a flute full and carried it around for some time before handing the half-full glass off to a waiter and refusing another. So that other guests could feel free to pick up and carry a drink, he'd murmured at the time, but there had been no more drinking on his part and she'd stuck to two drinks, although contrary to him she'd finished both. Waste not want not, and all that.

'So it's not that you don't drink.' She set her clutch on a side table and silently admired the sheer beauty of him in the lamplight. 'But rather that you don't drink when on duty.'

'Exactly. May I pour you a nightcap?'

She asked for limoncello. He opted for a Scotch that might have been older than her. Would they sit down to dissect the evening and predict tomorrow's headlines, was that how this went? Because, boring.

But he didn't start there. Instead he flung himself down in the middle of a sturdy love seat, set his drink down and beckoned her closer with the crook of his finger and a smile that the devil would have been proud of. The whole display was pure arrogance and pantomime.

She loved it. 'Very smooth.'

'The drink?' He made a fine show of taking a sip and then dangling the crystal tumbler carelessly from finger and thumb. 'Yes.'

'The undressing and making yourself at home too. Why don't you let me get your tie?' She made a great show of leaning over to gently pull it apart and then flip his collar up and slide the tie free of his very fine shirt. Tut-tut. The poor man's shirt buttons were positively strangling him, so she attended to them too. 'Is this what a valet would do for you?'

'No.'

Such a delicious rasp to his voice.

'How fond of that gown are you?'

'Extremely fond.' Didn't mean she had a burning desire to keep it on. 'Why?'

'Because I'd like you to sit with me.' He put the glass down and patted his well-formed thighs. 'On me…'

'Ride you?' He had the best ideas.

Crushed velvet seemed such a small price to pay for the pleasure of straddling firm thighs and putting her hands to a warm chest clothed in finest cotton. He kept his hands to himself and maybe he liked it when she tilted his head the better to brush her lips against his. She wasn't a dominant soul, not really, but this acquiescence of his was starting to work for her in ways that went straight to her centre, pulling and twisting and teasing, such a lovely, teasing mouth he had on him, and kisses that smiled.

Where was his tie when she needed it? But the two sides of his collar would have to do as she grasped the fabric and deepened the kiss, even as he shifted to press the steel of his erection against her heated folds. He'd been a cocky teen and for good reason, long and thick, and she couldn't help but set up a rhythm that pleased her. Tiny circles

against the generous wedge of him. 'I hope you remember how to use that,' she murmured against his
lips and brought forth another smile.

Sex could be teasing, and playful and fun before
turning white hot with passion. He'd taught her that
and she saw no reason to abandon such teachings
now. Sex could be urgent and messy or lazy and
sated. Never just the one thing, you had to direct it.
Feel your way. 'I remember you, you know. Your
kisses. Your hands. Vividly,' she murmured.

'You should. You had me at my best. Maybe not
my smoothest…' His fingers were feeling their way
beneath her panties right now, sliding into her with
unerring accuracy as his moistened thumb found her
nub and circled again and again. 'But definitely at
my most committed.'

There was nothing quite like a firm and knowing touch and none had ever been as knowing as
his. Truth to say, she'd never allowed it. For all her
hedonistic talents she'd never opened to any other
man the way she had to him and for a passionate
woman—which she was—it had been a very long
time between drinks. She was about to embarrass
herself, no question, what with his touch and his
scent and the whisper of stubble on his jaw doing
her in. 'We could slow down some.'

'Why?'

Because I'm almost already there, she could have
confessed.

Because my memories of what was and what is

are twining together to create an irresistible mix, she could have mentioned.

Because I'm not and never have been easy, she could have said, and it would have been the truth.

Only him.

Only this.

She closed her eyes and let him drive her higher, signalling her pleasure with drugging kisses, unable to stop her body from following where he led, but she wanted him sheathed in her when she crested.

'Put it inside.' Words she whispered as she fumbled to undo his belt and then the buttons—who did buttons with a member like his?—and then there was underwear and she nearly keened her relief when he halted his ministrations to lift his hips and push his clothes down and out of the way, and she knew exactly what to do with what was left.

Slowly, she positioned herself against his tip and bore down with a gasp. It was just as fulfilling as she remembered as he inched his way inside her... *slowly does it*...until they were a perfect fit. How? How did that fit where it did and still manage to feel so good?

'Size Queen,' he murmured, as if reading her thoughts, and maybe it was true.

'I've missed you *so much*.' And if that was a ridiculous reply he took as referencing his girth, well who was she to correct him?

'Missed you too.'

The things they'd learned together, about each

FREE BOOKS GIVEAWAY

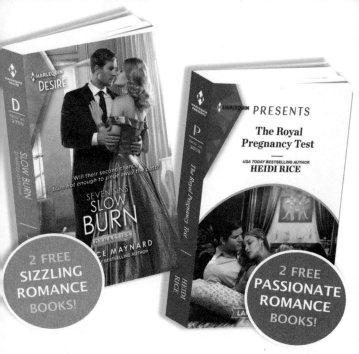

GET UP TO FOUR FREE BOOKS & TWO FREE GIFTS WORTH OVER $20!

We pay for everything!

YOU pick your books –
WE pay for everything.

You get up to FOUR New Books and TWO Mystery Gifts...absolutely FREE

Dear Reader,

I am writing to announce the launch of a huge **FREE BOOK GIVEAWAY**... and to let you know that YOU are entitled to choose up to FOUR fantastic books that WE pay for.

Try **Harlequin® Desire** books featuring the worlds of the American elite with juicy plot twists, delicious sensuality and intriguing scandal.

Try **Harlequin Presents® Larger-Print** books featuring the glamourous lives of royals and billionaires in a world of exotic locations, where passion knows no bounds.

Or TRY BOTH!

In return, we ask just one favor: Would you please participate in our brief Reader Survey? We'd love to hear from you.

This FREE BOOKS GIVEAWAY means that we pay for everything! We'll even cover the shipping, and no purchase is necessary, now or later. So please return your survey today.

You'll get **Two Free Books** and **Two Mystery Gifts** from each series to try, altogether worth over **$20**!

Sincerely

Pam Powers

Pam Powers
For Harlequin Reader Service

Complete the survey below and return t today to receive up to 4 FREE BOOKS and FREE GIFTS guaranteed!

▼ DETACH AND MAIL CARD TODAY! ▼

FREE BOOKS GIVEAWAY
Reader Survey

1   **2**   **3**

Do you prefer stories with happy endings?	Do you share your favorite books with friends?	Do you often choose to read instead of watching TV?
◯ YES ◯ NO	◯ YES ◯ NO	◯ YES ◯ NO

YES! Please send me my Free Rewards, consisting of **2 Free Books from each series I select** and **Free Mystery Gifts**. I understand that I am under no obligation to buy anything, as explained on the back of this card.

❏ **Harlequin Desire®** (225/326 HDL GQ4U)
❏ **Harlequin Presents® Larger-Print** (176/376 HDL GQ4U)
❏ **Try Both** (225/326 & 176/376 HDL GQ46)

FIRST NAME   LAST NAME

ADDRESS

APT.#   CITY

STATE/PROV.   ZIP/POSTAL CODE

EMAIL ❏   Please check this box if you would like to receive newsletters and promotional emails from Harlequin Enterprises ULC and its affiliates. You can unsubscribe anytime.

Printed in the U.S.A. ® and ™ are trademarks owned and used by the trademark owner and/or its licensee.

other, seemed to stand the test of time. That place at his jaw, just before his ear, that made him curse when she grazed it with her teeth and then soothed it with her tongue. The way he dived into a kiss and wouldn't be satisfied until they were both blue for breath and gasping at the end of it. The sheer joy of slick bodies pressing, pressing against each other, rise and fall, empires could fall in that moment and there would still be no stopping them. Rise and fall. Rise and fall and climb and plead and beg.

'I need—'

He knew exactly what she needed. Less clothing, more flesh, hands on her body and her nipple in his mouth. Just like that, yet it wasn't the way it had been all those years ago in the hunting cabin. They had plenty of time now and somewhere along the way he'd taken a masterclass in finesse.

Nothing between them but the air they breathed and the searching, seeking slide of flesh within flesh. The velvet of the couch beneath them. The dim light and the way his gaze didn't leave her face, fierce and glittering, and she wondered, with what little brain she had left, how she'd gone so long without this kind of connection.

Such a deliciously deep connection.

'Hello again,' she whispered against the curve of his neck, and prayed their indulgence wouldn't cost them as much as it had last time. 'Is this what you want from me?'

His answer was yes, and yes again as she set up

a tiny rocking motion with her pelvis that had him groaning and laughing and setting his busy hands to her hips and clamping her to stillness.

'Too soon.' And this time his kisses were set to soothe. 'Slow down. Long and slow, Angelique. I've waited so long. Let me learn you all over again.'

He stayed the night and most of the following morning.

And in this he was a man of his word.

He couldn't get enough of her.

Valentine knew he was ignoring the terms of their loosely discussed agreement—especially when it came to keeping Angelique separate from the duties imposed on him by the monarchy, but it was such a little transgression to begin with. He'd stayed overnight at the manor, again, and had a morning appointment with a charity he personally supported. He'd told her about it over breakfast and she'd seemed so interested in what they did, and what he did to amplify their reach, that he asked her if she wanted to come with him.

Foolish, foolish man, because it had quickly turned into a public relations disaster, and, in hindsight, Valentine took full responsibility. He hadn't briefed her properly, for starters. He hadn't told the organisers he was bringing a guest.

He'd sprung the trip on her one morning as he played house with her, his stomach full of bacon and mushrooms and sourdough toast, and his mind still clouded by their activities of the previous night. He'd wanted to stay with her just that little bit longer, eke out a couple more hours spent soaking in her warmth, so he'd asked her to accompany him on a job.

She'd been dressed too casually, for starters. Flat shoes, neat trousers, a collared cotton shirt with the sleeves rolled up to sit just below her elbows. No jewellery to speak of, except for the watch she wore on an everyday basis. The charity they had visited tackled adult literacy. As an adult for whom Thallasian was not her first language, Angelique had been genuinely interested in the classes and the teaching materials provided.

Her enthusiasm for their work had been everything he could have asked for.

When one of the organisers had asked if she minded being filmed reading from one of the beginner texts, she hadn't minded a bit and Valentine had nodded yes. She'd mangled the story, of course. Her spoken Thallasian was far in advance of her ability to read it. It was her fourth language behind her native Spanish, Liesendaachish and English.

The video had gone live on social media and the press had feasted on her ignorance.

Not only had the King's whore been shabbily dressed, she'd pimped an expensive watch brand she was ambassador for—thus monetising her association with His Majesty the King of Thallasia—and she had the reading skills of the average Thallasian eight-year-old.

All the good work of the charity had been buried beneath an avalanche of criticism, unsubtle innuendo about what the King saw in his foreign mistress, and the prediction that she couldn't possibly hold his interest for much longer.

All of it was his fault for deviating from the carefully curated script the palace had laid out for him.

Get your head out of the clouds and *protect* the woman, his sister had berated him, and rightly so.

Benedict—once upon a time the Crown Prince of scandalous headlines involving Angelique—had phoned to ask if Valentine had any other tips to impart when it came to ruining a woman's reputation. Not a good move on Benedict's part because it afforded Valentine the opportunity to vent about how little care Benedict and Carlos had had for Angelique's reputation—using her to hide their relationship behind for years and years, letting them say those things about her, and Benedict had said pot, kettle, black, and hung up on him.

Only to call back an hour later to say that he and Carlos had decided to grant a glossy magazine an interview in which they intended to emphasise Angelique's generosity and willingness to put her brother's happiness first as he navigated not only coming out but being in a serious relationship with a royal family member.

Not that Angelique would likely care one way or

another about the article, or any other articles written about her, Benedict had warned.

Angelique cared a great deal about what her tight circle of friends and family thought of her, and beyond that, people could say what they liked. She truly didn't care, and it wasn't a front, although it might have started out as a kind of defence.

And maybe that was a fine quality for a king's mistress to have, but Benedict rather thought not, which meant Valentine, and Benedict, and others around her needed to lift their game and protect what she would not. This was what Benedict had phoned to say before they'd embarked on their blame game.

And this time, Valentine listened intently, and after work that day, when he joined her for dinner and Angelique barely spared the articles a glance, he asked her why she wasn't more upset and settled back against the chair in the manor kitchen and listened.

'I have my work.' She swirled the burgundy wine around in her glass and took an appreciative sip before continuing. 'I've spent all day on this beautiful estate, largely cut off from the rest of the country, and my horses care nothing for the words of people who live to find fault. I have a wonderful life here.'

'The tabloids are calling you dim.'

'Do you think I'm dim? I truly hope not.' She shook her head as if to dismiss the notion. 'Me and my family were blooded in this type of warfare years ago and know to ignore it. It doesn't bother me. I expect no less from the press hounds of Thallasia. Do you truly expect them to love me? She studied him curiously. 'Because if you do, you're dreaming.'

'It truly doesn't bother you, this rubbish they print about you?' he asked.

'No. Does what they say about you bother you?'

'Yes. I have a team of people dedicated to ensuring that the bulk of my press stays favourable. I can do more good when I'm seen to be above reproach.'

She snorted inelegantly. 'I get it. I do. But your relationship with me is never going to be above reproach.'

'People accepted my infertility, my broken engagement and my desire not to marry. Not at first, this is true, but they're coming around to realising that my will to serve my country remains true. If we—I—made a point of emphasising the real you, maybe they'd accept you too.'

'You'd do all this groundwork for a fling?'

'What fling?' He might as well bury that notion along with every last remnant of his pride. 'I don't know about you, but this is the happiest I've ever been and it's because you're in my world. I want to continue with this…whatever it is that we're doing— do we really need to define it? But whatever it is, it's not a fling. You're important to me. The way Thallasia sees you is important to me.'

Now would be the time for Angelique to say the same to him, but she said nothing. Instead she raised her glass to her lips, but she was still here and listening and he came by his reputation for strong powers of persuasion honestly. 'To that end—

'What are they saying about me today?'

It was the first time he'd been interrupted in…for ever, and the hint of a smile on her lips suggested she probably knew that already. He picked up the paper in front of him and made a great show of shaking it out. 'You're about to reveal the whereabouts of the secret love child you bore me all those years ago.'

'I see.' She lowered her glass but kept her fingers on the slender stem. 'That's a new one. They're assuming your father wouldn't have taken care of that in the most brutal way possible. You lot have very short memories.' The minute she said it, her expression changed to one of contrition. 'Sorry. That comment was out of line. I don't equate your father with all Thallasians, you know. I don't see him in you.'

'Maybe that's because I've spent a lot of time and effort stamping him out. He's not a man I wish to emulate. His behaviour towards you all those years ago brought that home most vividly. Even so, I still see parts of him in me. My temper. My…arrogance. For all that I'm more aware of it than I once was, it still rises when I'm challenged.'

'Doesn't everyone's?'

'I would not know,' he murmured. 'People tend not to have temper tantrums when I'm around.' People were deferential to him. It came with the king thing and probably did him no favours at all. 'I don't need that from you. I like when we talk like this, when you interrupt my pontificating.' Hell yes, she *had* known exactly how that might wind him up, her smirk said as much. 'I need you to be able to speak your truth and not apologise for it—even if you're speaking ill of my father.'

She tossed her raven mane and fixed him with a haughty stare. 'I'll apologise if I want to, and don't you forget it. And now...' She flicked a quick glance at the tabloid on the table before pushing the mess aside and planting her pert behind in its place. 'If we've finished examining my press for the day, perhaps we might move on to other, more important matters. You could stop looking at the newspapers and destress instead.' A kiss for the edge of his lips, undemanding as far as kisses went, but with the promise of more if he wanted it. 'Would you like me to help you with that?'

'Absolutely, by all means, help me destress.'

Everything Angelique offered only served to make him hungrier for more of her. He resented having to parcel out his time with her like a miser, having to carefully vet where he could be seen with her, and even then the ludicrous articles about her just kept coming...

'But first I want you to consider doing an interview about literacy, about the languages you do speak, about the fact that you're unapologetically learning to read and write Thallasian. You can do it here, but the palace will style you and organise the interview.'

'About that arrogance,' she murmured, but he silenced her with a kiss.

'Please.' He who so rarely had to justify his demands.

'Why feed the beast? That article about me being dim will be forgotten soon enough. As for styling me, you need to stop thinking of my looks as something to be harnessed and used to make people like me. It doesn't work like that. Usually, it makes others wary or resentful.'

'A statement from you, then.' He could be flexible. 'The palace will release it.'

She 'hmm-ed' against his cheek. 'How about, "I'm working hard to improve my verbal and written Thallasian, and have already started using the learning strategies shared by the adult literacy teachers and students of Loannault Community House. Next time I attend, I hope they'll see an improvement." Will that do?'

'You're good at this.'

'For what? Staying on message?'

'For putting up with everything that comes of being seen with me.' He pulled away a little, the better to see her eyes. How could she stay so serene when strangers made it their mission to pick her apart in order to score a headline? But she didn't look stressed or indignant. She looked as if she'd put it out of her head altogether and moved on to contemplating far more favourable things.

Namely him.

One elegant eyebrow rose and her lips curved in a satisfied smile.

Definitely him. 'Am I wearing too many clothes?' he asked.

'In my considered opinion, always.'

She made him laugh, this woman others thought so far beneath him. She made him think there could be a safe place for him far away from palace doors, and he'd never thought that before.

'Shirt buttons. Hurry up.' She reached for the top one and set it free. 'Must I do everything?'

Could he ask to lie back and be loved by her? 'Is that an offer?'

Her fingers stilled on button three as she paused to glance at his face. 'Oh,' she said softly, as realisation kicked in. 'You'd like me to lead tonight.'

'Yes.' The minute she said it, he wanted exactly that. Ached for it. Longed to lay the burden of leadership at her feet, if only for a night, and if such a request made him weak, so be it. 'Please.'

She caught his lips in a kiss that plundered first and then promised heaven. Mischief lurked in the curve of her mouth and the way she nibbled at the bow of his upper lip. 'You realise Moriana's been telling me about the round room Sera set up for King Augustus. The one with the trapeze and the owls and the big round carpet and the bathing area? I say we start this pamper Valentine session in a bathroom. There's a big spa bath here off the main bedroom, and, while it's not big enough for two, there are water jets, there's a sitting step for any-one who doesn't intend getting in, and it won't take long to fill.'

Water had so often been his punishment when his late father had wanted to toughen him up or punish him. Perhaps this time it could soothe him. 'Is that so?'

'Mmm-hmm. So why don't we head that way—bring your drink—and let me see what I can do for you?'

He was shivering by the time he sank naked into the steaming, scented water but it wasn't from the cold. She'd lit candles and kept the lights low, and maybe for someone else it would be romantic, but the cavern beneath the palace had always been poorly lit too, the water running swift and black through what his father had euphemistically called a pool. A rock overhang had covered the mouth of the river at one end and a steel grate formed the other end of the pool, letting water through the grid but not a person, and it had been fun to be pinned against it when the river ran sluggish and peaceful, and no fun at all when the river became a torrent.

'No jets,' he murmured, when Angelique went to turn them on, and maybe that was him taking control again when he didn't mean to, but he couldn't stand the thought of them. Angelique didn't question his request, merely picked up a flannel, loaded it with soap scrub and began to wash him down. This he could do. This firm and thorough touch that became more massage than tease, and relaxed muscles he didn't know he had.

'Lean forward,' she instructed, so he did, allowing her to start in on his back, slow circular movements, and then she set the flannel and soap aside, sluiced him down with water from her cupped hands and then smeared those hands with oil and began rubbing the tension from his shoulders.

She'd had her hands all over him before, but he doubted she'd ever seen his back the way she could now, and he wondered whether the dim light would conceal his shame or not. He could barely feel the whip welts any more, where his father had broken the skin, but he'd been told they were still visible if one looked closely enough, silvery lines on otherwise smooth olive skin.

She dug her thumbs in and slid them up his spine, all the way to the base of his neck, and he shuddered again, leaving old memories behind in favour of groaning his appreciation.

'Who did this to you?' she asked finally.

'My father.'

'Why?' Straight to the point, no surprise at his words. Had everyone seen his father so much more clearly than him?

'I displeased him.'

Her hands worked him over, gentler than they had been. 'When you were a child?'

'Why does it matter?' Everything about those marks on his back shamed him. That his first stumbling steps towards being a man of honour had been met with a whip. That he'd been too surprised to defend himself. That Vala hadn't been able to meet his gaze as she'd tended him afterwards with salve she'd stolen from the kitchen's first-aid kit. 'It happened. It made me examine the kind of man I was and wanted to be. It made me seek my leadership role models elsewhere. In the armed forces for several years. In neighbouring monarchs and elder statesmen after that. I'm not proud of those whip marks on my back, don't get me wrong. But they forced a reckoning, not with my father, but within me. For that I'm grateful.'

She was silent for a long time after that, but her hands kept moving, and when more words came, they were halting. 'Valentine, did I cause this?'

'No.' He could say that with certainty, even if his liaison with her had been at the root of it. 'Let it go, Angelique. I've made my peace with them. There's no point reopening old wounds.'

She replied by crawling into the bath behind him and setting her lips to his scarred skin and he wanted to weep at her silent understanding. 'Relax,' she said. 'No more questions. Just feel.'

Not until every part of his body had been loosened did she urge him from the bath and towel him down and lead him to her bed. Fresh sheets and lazy kisses as he closed his eyes and let his hunger for her rise. Sank into her touch and let it build and build until he was a mass of writhing sensation and his head was filled with nothing but gratitude for every caress.

He'd never felt more naked than when, finally, she straddled him and took him in, took him apart, and in her own good time remade him.

He slept after that, fell hard and deep into oblivion, and when he woke and reached for her in the night she was there right beside him, warm and willing and this time he led. Giving back, getting lost all over again but he didn't care. It was too good and yet never enough and he prayed she would be strong enough to stay with him across the years and be content.

Or you could marry her and afford her the protections she deserves, a little voice whispered.

But that would be the end of her freedom, and for all that he was the son of a tyrant and a hard man in his own right, he wouldn't wish that role on her. This arrangement here was working for her. She had a career she could continue to grow and he had ready access to her, and if he missed her more and more whenever he was away from her, so be it. If the press flayed her for daring to claim some of his time, he had better get used to defending her.

'Be happy with me,' he whispered against her hair, big spoon to her little one, and she stirred in her sleep, and he stilled until she settled once more before adding a silent please.

Surely he could claim this small happiness.

Okay, not small, call it what it was. Surely, this

deep, all-encompassing contentment in his bones
and in his heart could be his.

Please.

CHAPTER NINE

THREE MONTHS LATER, happy beyond all reckoning, Angelique came to another reckoning while retching over the laundry sink because the smell of her morning coffee made her sick. It was the third time in a week, and the smart thing to do would be to swap out the coffee for a cup of something less fragrant, and she intended to, cross her heart. Morning sickness problem solved.

Morning.

Sickness.

'Madre de Dios.'

She couldn't be pregnant. Could she? Because Valentine couldn't have children and she sure as eggs wasn't sleeping with anyone else. Eggs. Terrible breakfast food that it was, she hadn't made any this morning for fear they would set her off. No food at all because she had a tummy bug.

Just a tummy bug.

She retched again, pitiful and groaning with the effort of bringing up nothing more than bile.

She reached for the tap and let the water swirl. She washed her mouth out and splashed her face and finally leaned back against the wet-room wall and dug in her coat for her phone. Stables first—she got hold of her head groom and told him she was ill and staying away from them all for a day or so. They talked about the exercise needs of various horses and her groom told her they had everything under control and to get well soon, and that he'd call again this afternoon.

The worry in his voice had not been feigned. She was a Cordova, and Cordovas had to be half dead before they neglected their horses. Three quarters dead, at the very least.

That or unexpectedly pregnant to an infertile king.

She called Luciana next, after having slid down the wall to sit on the floor. She had her forehead to her knees, the jodhpur material warm and familiar against her skin.

'Hey,' she murmured when Lucia picked up. 'Can you do me a favour?'

'It's not even six a.m.,' her sister grumbled. 'I can do you a favour by not yelling at you for waking me up. How does that sound?'

'Sorry. Very sorry.' She closed her eyes as nausea churned again. 'I'll call you back. Give me a time that's good for you.'

'What do you want?' Her sister's voice held a hint of worry in it now.

She took a deep breath, held if for a slow count of five and then let it back out. 'A pregnancy test.'

Silence.

'I'd buy one myself but if the press got wind of it...' She didn't want to think what would happen if the press got wind of it before she'd had a chance to speak with Valentine.

'How can you possibly be pregnant?' Lucia argued. 'You can't be.'

'I *know*. But it's been months since I last bled, and, while that's not uncommon if I work hard and drop weight, I have neither dropped weight nor worked myself ragged recently. My breasts are sensitive, my hair is thicker, and the smell of coffee makes me retch. Tell me that doesn't sound like I'm pregnant.'

'Are you glowing? Pregnant women glow.'

'Don't make fun of me, Lucia. Please. I think I'm pregnant, I'm terrified, and I need a pregnancy test. Or two. Maybe three in case I don't believe the results of the first two.'

'Oh, hell. How? No, scrap that question, I know how. But how the hell did they get Valentine's diagnosis so bloody wrong? Doesn't he have the best of the best physicians? If there'd been the tiniest chance of him siring an heir wouldn't he and the doctors have been all over that possibility?'

'You'd think so.' She didn't know what to think.

'Do you have a belly?'

'No!' Not yet. Did she? Riding horses all day

made a person toned enough that she would know. She ran a hand over the area in question. 'I don't think so? No one's said anything. But the breasts, Lucia. The breasts!'

'What about mood swings? Are you feeling all hormonal these days?'

Was she? Hard to say. She could be a little highly strung on the best of days. 'Nothing more than usual.' She tried to sound confident about that and vowed to ask her grooms if she'd been more difficult than usual recently. 'Can you post me a test? Or three?' Valentine had a permanent security detail at the manor these days, and he justified it because of the amount of times he visited. They also checked her mail. She'd have to hover and get the parcel before they did, but it could be done.

She was almost sure it could be done.

'No.' From her sister's mouth to her ears, and it shocked her into speechlessness. Lucia had always come through for her. 'You're not doing this alone. I'll be there by this evening and I'll bring a batch of tests with me.'

Inexplicably, her eyes filled with tears. 'I don't know what I'd do without you. I love you so much. You're the other half of my heart, with me every step of the way and I would be desolate without you. Desolate!'

Silence greeted her tearful declaration.

'Luciana?'

'Oh, my God, you're pregnant.'

* * *

The day passed excruciatingly slowly and when Luciana emerged through the airport arrivals door Angelique was hard pressed not to fling herself into her arms and drag her to the nearest restroom. Her sister took one look at her, enfolded her in a hug and muttered, 'Bathroom. Now.'

Being a twin with the near psychic ability to know what the other was thinking had never been more glorious.

They went into adjoining cubicles and Lucia passed a package full of pregnancy tests beneath the door before seeing to her own needs. If they were monitoring cubicles on film, a security person would likely be waiting for them when they exited. That was the thought she chose to occupy her mind as she peed on a stick and waited.

And then did it again.

Upon exiting, she met Lucia's eyes in the mirror and didn't have to say a thing.

'Dios mio.'

Oh, my God. Lucia had said it for her.

They ate a late meal at the village near the manor. Valentine rang, and, when he heard she was with Lucia, decided against coming over.

Luciana smirked as he told them to enjoy their catch-up and that he'd likely see them tomorrow. 'That man is scared of me. As he should be. When are you going to tell him?'

The food in her mouth suddenly tasted like ash.

'You should do it while I'm here.'

And have Lucia witness his disbelief and never, ever forgive him if things did, in fact, work out okay? 'I think it needs to be a private conversation.'

'Suit yourself.'

'Maybe I could do it by phone.'

'And deny yourself the look on his face or his temper while he sorts out other people's mistakes surrounding his diagnosis? That could work.'

But she did want to see his face, that was the problem. 'This arrangement that we have...it doesn't involve children. Valentine's not going to *want* a child.' And at her sister's raised brow. 'He's not going to want a child with *me*. If he's all fixed and fertile he'll be off to find a proper princess to marry. One his country will accept without reservation.'

'Why are you even with him if that's what you think he's going to do? Don't you trust him to do right by you at all?'

Angelique's hesitation spoke volumes. 'He's a king. I trust him to serve his country, first and always.'

'Then he's a fool.'

'Maybe so.'

Her sister eyed her speculatively. 'Would you marry him if he asked you to? Spend the rest of your life as a civil servant with pretty clothes and tiaras and a child who might one day sit on a foreign country's throne?'

She bowed her head and tried to picture all the rigmarole that happened every time they stepped out somewhere together multiplied a hundredfold. Every day planned down to the last second. Almost every evening spoken for in one way or another. Patronages and responsibilities eating into her time with the horses. The horses... The family business... Goodbye to all she'd worked for.

On the other hand, waking up to Valentine in bed beside her every morning was a vision she could embrace. 'I don't know. I doubt he'll ask.'

'Oh, he'll ask,' Luciana muttered grimly. 'What a mess.'

Angelique lowered her fork; she couldn't eat any more. Couldn't even take a sip of the wine Lucia had ordered for them both, just in case any reporters had spotted them. Champagne for breakfast and bottles of wine with every meal. Man-eating sirens, both. They had reputations to uphold.

'Eat,' Lucia urged, but she shook her head, tears threatening to fall, and if this emotional cresting and cratering was what she had to look forward to for the next six to nine months she'd be a wreck before the child even took its first breath.

And then a flash went off nearby, and her sister swore, and tossed her napkin on the table and rose, looking every inch the avenging devil. 'Let's get out of here.'

Heaven knew where that photo would end up. Probably in tomorrow's news cycle alongside a heading declaring her desolate because Valentine had tossed her over.

Which might just be true.

'Keys.' Angelique handed them over and let her sister drive them to the manor.

By the time the gate guard nodded to them and waved them in, she had herself under control and even managed a smile. Luciana went one better and lifted her finger from the steering wheel in acknowledgement, all smiles and credible good cheer.

All this luxury. All the beautiful pastures and training facilities for the horses were wholly dependent on the whims of a king who'd only ever taken up with her because he couldn't have children. The entire foundation on which they'd based their relationship lay in tatters at the feet of her newly pregnant self. 'I think I'll take that third test when we get inside. Just in case the other two were faulty.'

'And when you've done that, I'll give you the next three packets,' her sister murmured sagely.

'How many did you bring?'

'Twelve.'

Angelique huffed a laugh. Slight overkill, but, then again, one could never have too many pregnancy tests when carrying the bastard child of an infertile king. 'Thank you.'

'We'll figure it out,' her sister reassured her. 'We're Cordovas. We always do.'

Valentine strode towards the royal stables with his niece in tow and a spring in his step that had nothing to do with the perfect blue sky or the happily skipping Princess at his side, and everything to do with the woman they were going to meet. Ask him if happiness came in the shape of a woman and a year ago he would have said no. Ask him if contentment meant sharing a simple meal at a kitchen table and he would have asked why?

Why would a woman's smile and hot temper and sharp observations of the world around them energise him so?

But they did, and continued to do so in spite of so many around him hoping his fascination for Angelique Cordova would fade. He didn't shove her presence down anyone's throat these days. They'd agreed she would accompany him to one royal event each month and the rest he would attend alone. Enough to let people know they were still seeing each other. Little enough to keep the worst of the press hounds away from her. Meanwhile, behind the scenes, he and Angelique became ever more entwined. This latest project—a pony for his horse-obsessed niece—had without question required Angelique's expertise. She'd said to leave it with her, because she had a pony in mind but her father might take some convincing to let the little gelding go.

The cost of the ageing gelding had not been insignificant, even for him.

Alessandro, his stable master, had been disappointed it hadn't been a breeding mare, preferably in foal.

Angelique had laughed when he'd told her that,

and muttered, 'He can dream. He and my father are cooking up something between them, you know. Be prepared to open your wallet even more when they present it to you. That or bargain. You have a mare my father wants. Cordova bloodlines a few generations back. I tell you this to help you in your upcoming negotiations.'

He'd teased her about putting him before family and she'd huffed and told him loftily that she'd deny it with her dying breath, and then there'd been sex.

Which wasn't something he needed to be thinking about as he made his way into the stables, with Juliana skipping at his side.

Angelique was already there and so was the horse, and there was no contest as to which of them drew his attention first. Call it a kink but he loved seeing this woman in shiny black riding boots, tight jodhpurs and that little collared work shirt with the silhouette of running horses and mountains making up the bottom third of the shirt. He wondered who had thought it better to put the picture low on the hip area rather than across the chest. Regardless, it drew his eye to the perfection of the body beneath.

'Afternoon, Horsemaster Cordova,' he said for Juliana's benefit. 'What have we here?'

'Your Majesty, Princess—may I introduce you to Girar? Although in English we call him Twist. When he was a little foal he used to turn and turn and turn.'

'Girar,' said Juliana, mangling the pronunciation, but Angelique nodded.

'Almost. You want a soft G and to cut off the R. Chop!' Another hand motion. Her hands often spoke for her. 'Girar. Say it.' And when Juliana did... 'Yes! Again. And again. That's it. You learn very quickly. He will like you, I know it.'

He hadn't expected her to have so much time for Juliana after her comments on not being cut out for motherhood. But his niece was entranced, and Angelique seemed equally happy to lavish attention on the girl.

'Shall I tell you a secret?' Angelique continued. 'All the children of the grooms in our Spanish stables get to learn from Girar. They are put on the back of the horses at a very young age, of course, but from ages six through to eight, they get him. And do you want to know why?'

His niece nodded, eyes shining.

'Because he is the best. If you lose a stirrup he will stop. If he's going too fast and you clutch at his mane, he will stop.' She suited mime to words and made his niece laugh. 'If you yell *para* really loud Girar will stop.'

'You taught the horse Spanish verbal commands? Not English?'

Angelique met his gaze and shrugged. 'Girar is one of our best. Hand-picked, hand-reared, and countless hours of training have gone into him. More than our usual standard of excellence. Normally we keep our best.' She dug into her pocket, produced a slightly crumpled, folded sheet of paper and handed it to Juliana. 'The boy who learned to ride on him most recently wrote you a note. It's in Spanish so you might need help reading it, but it tells you all the things Girar likes best. The boy is of the opinion only very special people are worthy of this pony, and I quite agree.'

'I'll write to him,' Juliana promised solemnly. 'I'll draw him a picture of Girar doing all his favourite things.'

'He'd like that.'

'Come,' Valentine commanded. 'Let us see this paragon of equine perfection that we are so very lucky to receive. Can he be used for polo at all?'

Angelique snorted. 'Are you deliberately trying to insult me?'

'No?' He hadn't been. Had he? 'I'm merely wondering how far his training extends beyond teaching people to ride.'

'Trust me, the horse knows the difference between a learner rider and a professional. You want to play polo on him, he will not disappoint. Careful, though. He turns on the head of a pin.'

The horse was perfectly formed, superbly conditioned and altogether happy to be fussed over by an enchanted little girl.

'He has a beautiful temperament,' she said as they stood back and watched Juliana brush the horse, under Alessandro's watchful tuition. 'He really is the best of our best for this purpose.'

'Thank you.' He'd asked for a horse and expected

a good one. He hadn't expected quite this level of sacrifice in order to accommodate him. 'Have you eaten?' She often didn't stop for food once she started her workday. He didn't know how she did it.

Her stomach chose that exact moment to betray her with a loud rumble, but she countered with a grimace. 'You had to talk about food. I'm not hungry. Really.'

'You sure about that?'

'Very.' She seemed subdued now that Juliana was otherwise occupied. 'Look, can we talk privately? I want to give Juliana a lesson on the horse but after that, can I come and find you?'

Something was wrong. And it wasn't that he read other people particularly well, but he knew what contentment looked like on her these days and this wasn't it. 'All right. Mind if I stay and watch the lesson?'

'Would it matter if I did?'

'Is there something wrong?' Might as well be direct.

'God,' she muttered. 'I just—' He suddenly found himself with an armful of woman who clung to him as if she'd never see him again after this. She trembled in his arms, her face buried somewhere in his chest, and he hoped to God the choked noise she made was a laugh and not a sob, because a crying Angelique would render him utterly lost.

'Any time.' He tightened his arms around her. 'You can just—any time.'

There was the laugh he'd been hoping for, and if it was a little bit wet, he was all for ignoring it. 'Let me get Girar's saddle and bridle and this excited little girl sorted and then let's do that again.'

He let her go reluctantly, aware of several pairs of eyes upon them. They normally didn't do displays of affection in public. Standard protocol for him, no matter what kind of relationship he might be in. Self-preservation for her, because the last thing she needed was to draw attention to all the ways she wasn't a suitable paramour for a king. She walked a fine line between ignoring the judgment of others and accepting that the easiest pathway to acceptance of her position in his life was to keep her head down.

Not since the literacy reading had she put a foot wrong, and, of all the stories about her wild, wild ways, not one of the people involved had a bad word to say about her.

The polo player who, when asked about his debauched weekend with her, laughed himself to tears before saying she was an absolute slave-driver and his arse would never be the same again, but his forward game was one hundred per cent better for knowing her. The soccer player she'd spent a weekend with, helping his four-year-old daughter overcome her fear of horses. The racing-car driver who'd wined and dined her, and had, on their second date, introduced her to his *nonna* who'd promptly forbidden him to corrupt her because she was far too good for the likes of him. She still kept in touch with the *nonna*, and with the driver, even though he was now happily married to someone else.

The more the press dug, the more the picture emerged that the Cordova family as a whole were tight-knit, supremely loyal to each other, and had a habit of collecting a wide circle of friends and keeping them. 'Go do your work. I'll wait.'

All she'd done was buy herself some time. Angelique smiled absently at Valentine's earnest young niece, and then shook her head to clear it of all thoughts of babies and betrayal. Right now, she held an eager young girl's heart in her hands and that was what she should be concentrating on. Quietly, Angelique began to explaining Girar's regular routine, and showed Juliana how to get the horse to lower his head so a not-so-tall person could put his bridle on and do it up without assistance. She put the girl on the horse and walked along beside them as they walked a lap of the round yard, her instructions warm and clear as she ran Juliana through lesson number one when it came to riding a Cordova pony, and all the while Valentine watched them from a distance, radiating a warmth and approval she could feel from anywhere in the training yard.

Maybe he'd understand. Maybe he'd realise that it was no one's fault and perhaps even think it a miracle that she was pregnant at all. Maybe he'd want her and the baby both, and Valentine would gain an heir even as she lost the lifestyle she'd worked so hard to build. Either way, with a pregnancy now in play, her work with the horses would soon be restricted to teaching and advising rather than riding.

Maybe—if wishes counted for anything—happiness would ensue.

She had the patience and enthusiasm reserved for only the finest of teachers. Valentine watched as his niece soaked up the attention like a sponge, her riding confidence improving a hundred times over as Angelique set about building trust between rider and horse. Angelique was good with children, generous and inspiring, and he wondered why that surprised him so much. She'd indicated so early on that having children of her own didn't interest her. She was with *him* now and knew full well he could not oblige her with that. She'd made her choice.

And still…

Watching her with Juliana made his heart ache, just a little.

His sister appeared beside him and together they watched the lesson in silence for several more minutes as Angelique ran through the commands for the horse to stop.

'This is the wildly expensive pony you're spoiling my firstborn with?' his sister asked finally.

'Not just your firstborn.' It was for his younger nephews too, never mind that they were still too young for the saddle. They'd grow. 'It's for all of them.' He tried another tack. 'And you too.'

Vala snorted inelegantly. 'You don't fool me, you know. Never have, never will.' She eyed the horse some more. 'He's well trained, I'll give you that. Is Angelique staying on for dinner? And if so, are you both dining with us or would you like me to tell the staff to provide a table for two in your quarters this evening?'

'Not sure yet.' Angelique hadn't exactly jumped at the idea of food. 'But I'll let you know.'

'She's welcome at my table. Just so *you* know.'

It was quite the acknowledgement. His sister's acceptance of Angelique into their inner circle. 'Thank you.'

She shrugged. 'How long will the lesson go on for? Because if you're waiting for my daughter to get sick of riding her new pony, you'll be waiting the rest of the day. More to the point, I need my daughter back. Her tutor's waiting.'

Ah. His habit of collecting Juliana whenever he had a spare moment to spend on her was beginning to rub his sister the wrong way. Easily fixed. 'Okay, ladies. Time's up. Juliana, you've other lessons to see to.'

Getting the child off the horse wasn't hard once she spotted her mother. He watched them return towards the castle, his solemn little niece talking nineteen to the dozen, and he didn't regret spoiling her one little bit. Not in this way, given all the extra tutoring in place now that the child was in line to inherit the throne. Angelique handed the horse off to Alessandro and he walked up to join them. 'Very instructive,' he offered.

'I hope so.' She seemed calmer now. Less agitated.

'Vala has invited us to dine with her and her family this evening, should you decide to stay on.'

'Oh.' She looked trapped, hunted. 'That's very kind of her.'

'Or we could dine in my quarters. It's not a big deal.'

She allowed him a tight smile. 'Let's talk first.'

But she didn't seem to have anything at all to say as they strode beneath the deep blue sky towards the palace. He took her through the back entrance to his quarters, up three flights of steps carved into stone and circling round and round until they reached a door that led directly into his bedroom via a hidden passageway and wall panel.

She stepped through and looked around, then looked back towards the tunnel that led to the stairs. 'Handy,' she murmured.

'Shall I send for refreshments?'

'I'm probably not staying.'

'Any particular reason why?'

She nodded, took a deep breath. 'I'm pregnant.'

'Excuse me?'

'Pregnant.'

He had no words.

'To you,' she added and lifted her chin.

'That's impossible.'

'Well, clearly it's not!'

But he couldn't comprehend a word she was saying. He turned away, a hand to his hair, and began to pace.

'I know what you're thinking,' she murmured.

'You have no damn idea what I'm thinking.' He *wasn't* thinking. His brain had stopped, hung up on that one little word. He couldn't… It wasn't… His.

'Who is he?' He saw her wince out of the side of his eye and he didn't care. How could she possibly think to fool him?

'You.' With only the barest tremble to testify to the lie. 'I don't know how far along I am—I haven't seen a doctor yet, but there's no other man in my life. It *has* to be yours, and I'll take any kind of DNA test you like in order to prove it. Whether you want to claim it as yours is the bigger question.'

But he was nowhere near accepting her words at face value. 'I'm not fertile.'

She shrugged with a helplessness he'd never before seen, her body suddenly too slender for him to even contemplate her carrying a child. His child. 'I don't know what to say to you,' she offered. 'You said you couldn't have children and I believed you. Why would you lie? We didn't use protection because of that very reason, yet here I am. Expecting. Take the test again.'

'*You* take the test again,' he shot back.

'I have. Too many times and the result never changes. *I'm pregnant!*'

'Keep your voice down!'

He couldn't look at her, couldn't stop running his hands through his hair and if it had been long enough to grab fistfuls and pull he'd doubtless be doing that too. How could his physicians have got it so wrong? Weren't they supposed to be the best? Had it all been some kind of plot to unseat him? A mix-up with the results? How the hell could a bunch of experts get it so wrong? 'You're sure about the pregnancy?'

'I took a pharmacy test.'

Bah. 'It's wrong.'

'Six of them. And while it's true I haven't seen a doctor yet, that's only because I wanted to do you the courtesy of telling you first.'

'It's not mine.' How could it be? He came to a halt in front of her. 'Whose is it? One of your grooms? One of my guards? One of your polo-playing swains?'

She held his gaze but he couldn't hold hers. 'Is that what you want me to say?' she asked at last.

'I want the truth!' he spat, hot temper getting the better of him.

'And when it turns out to be yours? What then? Or can your tiny brain not think that far ahead?'

He couldn't stay; he had to get out of there before the shadow of his father rose up and pushed him towards behaviours he'd sworn never to emulate. 'Stay here.' While he headed for the door. 'If you leave, I will hunt you down.'

He didn't wait for her reply as he left the room and started calling for guards. Two for the door to his quarters. Another for the door to the hidden stairs that would take her to the garden. God only knew when he'd feel calm enough to return and she wasn't going anywhere.

'Where are you going?'

He heard her words but his stride didn't slow. 'Away from you.'

Down, down, past the dungeons to the underground caverns where his forefathers had discovered a river and waterfall, where the water would be icy cold and exactly what he needed and where his body would take a pounding beneath the forceful torrent and if he let the current take him he would wash up against the grate. If he fought the current and swam, his body would soon exhaust itself but his tension and anger would be gone, buried beneath the primal urge to simply survive. He could thank his father for this particular coping method. He'd been a child when his father had pushed him to the edge of the water-fall and ordered him to jump.

Because he was too hot-headed and undisciplined even then.

Jump and cool the hell off.

The icy water helped. The pounding water beneath the fall pummelled his temper into submission, although there would be bruises tomorrow and an aching body to go with them. It would give him something to hold onto besides anger.

'There are easier ways to die, you know.' The voice was light and languid, but the mind behind it was sharper than most people knew. He turned to face his sister—younger than him by mere minutes. She'd escaped their father's notice and much of his wrath simply by being beautiful, outwardly obedient and second in line to the throne rather than first. 'Our head of security tells me there's a Cordova locked in your bedroom.'

'Locked is a strong word.'

'Is there another word you'd like me to use? Are you sure you don't want to get out of the water yet?'

'Positive.'

'Because your skin is turning blue.'

'Five more minutes.'

'That's four minutes too many. Because I really don't want to be crowned Queen any time soon— any time at all, if we're being honest.'

'Angelique's pregnant.'

Valentine had the dubious pleasure of seeing his sister rendered speechless.

'She says it's mine.'

'And you believe her?'

God help him, he wanted to. 'She says she'll take any test I want her to have.'

His sister began to smile. 'But what marvellous news.'

'Really? *Really?* Angelique Cordova—a woman

Thallasia loves to hate—is having my baby and you call that a *good* thing?'

'Don't *you*?'

'Yes. God forsake me, I want this so much it hurts.' He closed his eyes and stuck his head beneath the fall of water again. Fear and anger and hope and tears and pain, and this time he let it all come out with an animal roar.

Then he felt a slender hand wrap around his biceps and pull, hard, and he opened his eyes to find his sister, fully dressed and soaking wet, tugging him towards the edge of the pool.

'I swear, people who say you got all the brains and I got all the beauty got it wrong,' she muttered. 'I've always been of the opinion that we're both too stupid for words. Hoist me up.'

He hoisted her up.

'It's simple,' she said from the edge of the pool as she reached down to haul him up beside her, and he tried to help himself out, he really did, but he barely had the strength for it. Maybe she'd been right to urge him out of the water, not that he'd ever tell her that. Not that he needed to say it, given the way he was gasping and shivering, and, yes, slightly blue.

'What's s-simple?' he chattered.

'The solution. Marry the woman you've never stopped loving, cherish the child you've created together, and close ranks in such a way as to protect them both until there comes a time when our misguided public value Angelique as much as you do.

It'll happen eventually, and probably sooner than you think if she gives you an heir.'

'If they believe it's mine.'

'Like you said, there are tests for that. They'll believe once they're forced to. Look at what our beloved public think of me. At the beginning of the year I was nothing more than a faded socialite bird-brain. Don't look at me like that, you know that's what they thought. And I have changed not one hair on my faded socialite head, yet all of a sudden I'm a fount of wisdom, fortitude and ageless beauty. The point is, you want this, don't you? If you could have any woman at your side, mother to your children, who would it be but her?'

'And what will I woo her with exactly? A public who is going to crucify her for her wild reputation—'

'Augustus of Arun married a *concubine*. How, exactly, is this any worse?'

'And she's a foreigner.'

'Cas's foreign Queen can guide her through the worst of it. And I can… I don't know…teach her how to handle your moods.'

'I'm not moody.'

'Please.' She made the most dismissive noise she could. 'You put me to shame.' His sister reached for his hand. 'Here you are with the gift of family right in front of you—and all you need to claim it is a willing heart, an *open* heart, and a thimbleful of un-derstanding and instead you choose punishing rage?'

'I'm not *choosing* it. I came down here to get rid

of it! Don't you understand? All those bits of him that are in me, this is where I come to drown them, so that I can go back up those stairs and offer a terrified mother-to-be my support with an open heart!'

Rage at his sister. Rage at the hand life had dealt him and the pressure to perform to standards he could never quite reach. Just rage. 'I don't even know if Angelique wants this child. It wasn't exactly planned. What if she says no to everything? To me.'

Now his sister was turning away from him, standing and walking over to the nearby pile of towels, and then she was back with a towel that she wrapped around his shivering frame and holding him tight and he closed his eyes and took comfort from the only person who'd always had his back—even when he sometimes hadn't been able to see it.

'How can I help?' she murmured gently. 'What do you need me to do?'

'Just…' He had no idea. 'If it doesn't go smoothly. If Angelique says no, and I start to turn into someone you don't like… If I start behaving like him… our father. Protect her.'

'I can,' she murmured. 'I will.'

CHAPTER TEN

IF ANYONE HAD asked Angelique how she'd thought her meeting with Valentine would go and they'd said, he's going to lock you in his quarters and walk away, she'd have dismissed it as crazy talk, and yet here she was. All locked in, with guards at all the entrances, and quite decidedly alone.

Valentine's suite consisted of a bedroom decked out in dark blues and deep brown mahogany, a white marble bathroom, a dressing room the size of an average home and a sitting room full of books, several deep-seated library chairs and a sideboard laden with sliced fruits, nuts, pastries, water and juice. The food had arrived ten minutes ago, when she'd also been told that His Majesty would be with her soon. Trying to brush past the guard had resulted in him crowding her deftly back inside the room and closing the door. Yelling and banging on the door had brought a staff member with more food and a calming tea—none of which she'd touched.

The huge arched windows did not open. If there

was another secret passageway—and what respectable king's bedroom didn't have more than one secret exit?—she had yet to find it. Valentine showed up five minutes later, his hair damp and his dark eyes raking her from head to toe. 'You left me locked in here to go for a *swim*?' she asked incredulously. He'd barely stepped inside the door, but she couldn't help but lash out. Fear and anxiety were riding her too hard.

'Needs must.' He surveyed the groaning table of untouched food. 'You haven't eaten.'

She laughed, tightly incredulous. 'Help yourself.'

He did just that, but not before handing her a sheet of thick, creamy coloured paper with a crest embossed on the top. 'Sign this.'

'What is it?' She couldn't read the language but a signature had already been scrawled on one side of the paper.

'Our wedding contract.'

He took his time spreading soft cheese on crusty bread, and topped it with a slice of fresh fig. 'Our what?'

'Dated today. There's no other way.'

'There's not marrying you. That's definitely an option.'

'You are sadly mistaken.'

'You can't just take what you want!' she snapped. 'There are rules. Laws.'

'And they will favour me.' He shrugged. 'If—as you say—the child is mine, you're carrying a future heir to the Thallasian throne, provided the baby is born within wedlock.' He smiled crookedly, wholly without mirth. 'Sign the papers. You're not leaving until you do.'

'Valentine, please. We do have other options.'

'What? Squirrel you away somewhere until you have the child? Pretend it doesn't exist? Adoption? Abortion? Letting a child of royal blood be born outside wedlock? I will tolerate none of those options. You will give me an heir. I will give you a crown and a lifetime of service. You lose—don't think I don't know that. Welcome to royal life.'

'Walk away,' she challenged him doggedly. She'd seen his utter disbelief and horror at the news they'd conceived a child together. He hadn't believed her. Hadn't wanted to believe her, and now all of a sudden he wanted to marry her?

'No.'

'You don't want this. *I saw you lose your mind at the thought.*'

'I found it again.'

'You can't possibly want to marry me. Your people will never accept me.'

'We'll see.' He ate the tiny snack he'd created, his manners neat, his hands already busy creating the next.

'Valentine, think.' She marshalled her arguments. 'You can have a proper wife, one who could help you rule—like Moriana does Theo, or Sera with the King of Arun. I'm not trained to do this. I know about horses. I won't do you any good.'

He ate again, poured a glass of water and then another and kept her waiting. 'Drink?' he asked finally.

'I don't want to be your brood mare.'

He picked up a plump date. Ate it.

'I am wholly unsuited to be the mother of future rulers!'

'You wouldn't be the first.' He looked at her, his lips twisted in a bitter little smile. 'C'mon, Angelique. I'm not a magician. I can't make your pregnancy unhappen, even if I wanted to—which given my circumstances I sure as hell don't. This is a gift for me. A second chance at a role I thought lost to me for ever. Did you seriously think I wouldn't take it?'

'If it turns out that you test fertile again—which you must be—you can marry well and have children you actually want. Why stick with me?' She voiced her deepest fear and watched as he went pale and his eyes glittered, first with shock and then thinly hidden fury.

'Is that truly what you think of me?'

'No!' Yes. 'Maybe.' Honesty was important. 'I think getting me pregnant with your child is not an outcome you would have wanted for your country.'

He turned away, jammed his hands into the pockets of his trousers and began to pace. 'Maybe you're right. But Valentine the man is ecstatic. You at my side and a family we've created—it's been my go-to fantasy for more years than I care to confess, so don't you dare think I don't want this. Us. A baby. I just never thought I could have it. Never dared reach for it might be a better description, but you're here for the taking, you *and* a chance at fatherhood. We've been happy these past few months, haven't we? I know I have. Marry me and we can continue with that. What's stopping us?'

She had to laugh at his arrogance. 'Your crown?'

He waved a hand. 'The people of Thallasia got over my inability to produce an heir. What's to say they won't honour you for giving me one?'

'Or call me a liar, you a dupe, and the child some-one else's—no matter what the tests say.'

'Are we caring about that?'

'Aren't you?' Hard to believe he wouldn't.

But he shot her a glance and just kept pacing. 'I've been emasculated, called suicidal, and my rule has come into question—all in the last few months. If some want to add cuckolded husband to that list, let them. I want a real marriage with you. Your passion, your anger, your problems and your dreams—I want it all. In return you get me and all my flaws exposed for you to see. In this we would be equal. I'll do my best to be a good father and husband. You will have horses. Helpers. Access to your family. Things to help you and our child be happy. It wouldn't be like it was during my father's reign. You have my word.'

'Where did you go? When you left me just now? What did you do?'

'As you say, I went for a swim to cool down and clear my head. And I have.'

Which was all well and good to say, but whether he really had or not was anyone's guess. 'You're sure you wouldn't like to, oh, I don't know, sleep on it? Take advice? Wait?' She stared at the blurry words on the paper. 'I can't even read this.'

'Turn it over. It's repeated in English on the other side.'

It was a simple enough contract. His offer of marriage, signed and witnessed. Her acceptance, still to be signed and witnessed. 'Is this even a legal document?'

'It is.'

'I'll bear witness.' The voice from the doorway came from Valentine's twin, a woman reputed to be flighty and none too smart. A woman obsessed with beauty and fashion and maintaining a perfect complexion. Except that wasn't how Angelique remembered Vala at all. Instead she remembered a girl who'd held her tongue when her brother had fallen for the stable girl. The sister who'd covered for her brother's unexplained absences more than once. A young woman who'd been outclassed on the polo field nine times out of ten but who'd taken her falls and got back up and dusted herself off with a sigh or a sob, and then gone to tend her horse, no matter her backside covered in grass stains or her hair full of dirt or the waiting stable hands whose job it was to care for the horses. She was not what the public made her out to be, this woman. Not by a long way. 'Hello, Angelique. Has he convinced you of his undying devotion yet?'

Um...

'Give it time,' Vala said into the silence. 'Do I need to witness this signature or not? I'm on a schedule.'

'I'm not signing it.'

'And I'm not leaving your side until you do,' he said.

Valentine had a pen. Inside pocket of his perfectly cut blazer. He held it out to her in silent challenge and she crossed her arms and stared him down. 'At least wait until you know it's yours. Get the tests done. Go see a doctor so you know what's going on with your *health*. Why did they call you infertile in the first place?'

'I fell ill last year with a childhood illness I had no immunity to. I recovered. My sperm count did not.'

'Can your fertility come back?'

'They said not.'

'Not ever?'

'Do you think either of us would be in this position had they said yes?'

No, no they would not. He would never have spent his royal sperm so unwisely if he'd thought his fertility might come back over time. 'I don't know what to say.'

'Say yes and sign the paper,' he urged.

'No. Can't we just…?'

'Just *what*?'

Frustration lit his words.

'Just wait and get the tests done and then *think* about this a little bit more.' She glanced at the paper he wanted her to sign. 'See if we can come up with a solution that isn't so…so…'

'Permanent?' He sneered. 'You're having my child. What the *hell* did you expect?'

She wrapped her hands tightly around her waist and looked away, unable to bear the confused despair in his eyes. 'I didn't ever expect to be in this position. Actually.'

And wasn't that the long and short of it?

'Right, well.' Vala clapped her hands as if to banish the heavy sorrow in the air. 'Leaving the paperwork and wedding plans aside, for now, let's bring a medical team in to examine both of you, shall we?'

'Not the usual ones,' Valentine warned her, and her schoolmarmish expression softened.

'I quite agree. Not the same set of incompetent, addle-headed buffoons you dealt with before—of that I'm sure.'

They believed her. Oh, he hadn't at first, but here he was now willing to marry her before he was even sure the baby was his and that had to count for something, didn't it?

Vala turned towards her. 'Angelique, I'll have a room made up for you—'

'She's staying with me.'

'I thought I'd head back to the manor.' Might as well put it out there as an option.

'I don't think you quite understand.' Valentine's voice came hard and implacable enough for her to glance up, only to be immediately ensared by his unfathomable black gaze. 'Until you sign that piece of paper, you're not going anywhere.'

Dinner was served in Valentine's quarters. A succulent roast with tender roasted vegetables and delicately buttered beans. Angelique barely ate any of it. Valentine's impeccable manners ruled every interaction, no sign whatsoever of the playful, laughing man who felt comfortable enough with her to truly let his guard down. No wryly revealing comments about the global news of the day. No snippets of personal information, sparingly spoken, but she'd hoarded them carefully and when bundled together they'd revealed a picture of a smart, passionate man with a deeply playful streak that he only allowed close friends and family to see.

Painstakingly built over that deeply private core was an impenetrable public persona of stern politeness, and it was this he showed her now. Asking her how her food was and did she need any additional fixings. Opting against having a glass of wine himself because she was not drinking or for some other reason he didn't care to share with her. Mentioning how pleased he was with Girar, the horse she'd delivered for his niece. Saying out of the blue, 'You're good with children.'

It was enough to make her fork clatter against the fine bone-china porcelain of the plate, and she winced, and muttered sorry, because clearly her table talk and manners were no match for his, and she couldn't read him at all. He probably had no idea what she was thinking either and it was all so wrong that she wanted to weep.

'Will you show me that place where you swam, earlier?' she asked after dinner, and it was partly because she wanted to get out of his suite and partly because walking, or swimming, might give them something to do besides brood and grow ever more distant with each passing minute.

She'd never been more grateful for the massive vastness of palaces as he led her down through the levels, past the storage cellars in the kitchen and lower still until they came to a door that pushed inwards into deep inky blackness. The flick of a switch revealed dozens of wall sconces, a long and skinny natural cave, and a turbulent, fast-flowing river running from one end of it to the other, entering through huge iron grills that someone small enough could probably pass through. Rough-hewn steps led to and from each end of the pool, only it wasn't like any pool she'd ever seen, it was a torrent. '*This* is where you swim?'

'It's more appealing on a good day.' He stood to

one side of her, watching the water. 'Some days it can be quite gentle.'

'Are there things in it? Fish?' Sharks… Bodies… Lost city of Atlantis…

He shrugged.

'And you swim in this? Just to be clear.'

He ran his hand around the back of his neck and shrugged again. 'I was six the first time my father brought me here. It was two days after my mother had died and I was too quiet and withdrawn for his liking. He told me to strip down to underwear and took me to the edge of those steps over there. Said she was dead but I was still alive and he would have no more moping from me and that I needed to toughen up. He said swim. And he pushed me in.'

She gasped. Couldn't help but cover her mouth.

'It was worse than it is now and by the time I'd surfaced I was halfway down the cave. I tried swimming to the side but ended up pinned against the exit grid before I got there. It was hell getting over to the steps and out of the water but I did it, and then I lay there on my back and I laughed, with my body full of endorphins, and I laughed, because it was either that or cry and I sure as hell didn't want to be thrown in again. My father seemed pleased with me.'

He couldn't be serious.

But he was.

And Angelique bit her lip and with it her horrified protest and tried her best to understand this complex, deeply wounded King.

'My father thought he was toughening me up. From my perspective, I'd discovered a whole new way to deal with emotions that were too big for me to hold inside. Grief, rage, isolation. A boy in a towering temper went into the water at that end, got pummelled by fear, and came out the other end calm again with all those dark, destructive emotions washed away.'

'That's horrific.' She had to say it.

'Works for me.' He straightened and turned to look her dead in the eye. 'I'm sorry I reacted badly to your news. That's not who I want to be.'

Such honesty demanded an equally honest reply. 'As a child my passions ruled me completely. I was so highly strung that sometimes my presence alone could upset the horses. The number of times my father ordered me out of the stables to go and sit on that rock till I'd cleared my mind...' She shook her head, remembering. 'But meditation never completely worked for me, and I doubt your river swims will either. Right now I have all these feelings churning around inside me with nowhere to go. The thought of marrying you scares me. I'd be such a liability.' She turned away, couldn't even hold his gaze.

And then he stepped up behind her, close enough that she could feel the heat of his chest through the layers of his clothes and hers. His hands settled lightly on her shoulders, his thumbs rubbing faint circles into the back of her neck. Too tentative for a massage. His touch had never been tentative before and it was just one more reminder of the way things had changed with the creation of a child.

Where was the joy?

'I never meant to trap you,' he offered quietly. 'I only ever wanted to love you.'

A sob rose up and tore through her throat, and then another, and then she cried, hard and ugly, and he turned her around and wrapped her in his arms where she repaid his steadfast support by drenching his shirt in a waterfall of tears. He held her until she was all cried out. Until she felt as if she'd swum that pitch-black river at her back and crawled up those jagged, wicked-looking stone steps, exhausted and empty.

'Right. So. Each to their own.' He put a finger beneath her chin and tilted her head until she met his gaze head-on. 'Feeling better yet?'

'Yes.' *Dios*, this man. 'Yes.'

Angelique never expected Valentine to be the one to break the news of her pregnancy to her father, but he was. She hadn't expected him to return to the manor with her, but he did. She couldn't sit without him asking her if she needed some food, or a drink, or a pillow for her back. She couldn't work in the stables without him ordering grooms to do her work. He stayed with her for days, no mention of his own work, as he not so subtly fortified the security around the estate.

Vala had indeed arranged a raft of medical specialists to attend them both. Angelique had been poked, prodded and had undergone a paternity test and the results had confirmed what she already knew. The baby was Valentine's.

As for Valentine's medical tests, they told him his viable sperm count remained next to non-existent, but there were clearly some that could... One that had...

She had an ultrasound done, with Valentine present, and she had to laugh because although she wasn't as far along as she'd thought—eight weeks or so rather than twelve—she'd be getting bigger in a hurry.

She was having twins.

If she thought Valentine fussed over her *before* he heard this news, it was nothing compared to his compulsive desire for her to be seated on a chaise longue for ever, with a bunch of grapes in hand, *after* he realised she was eating for three.

She bluntly told him that maybe he didn't have to return to the manor to tuck her in each night, or bear witness to her pale face and uneasy stomach of a morning.

His sister was pushing for him to break the news of his impending fatherhood and upcoming nuptials. 'Get out there and sell it,' she'd pleaded during her last visit. 'God help me, Valentine, you're not doing yourself any favours by neglecting your duties and holing up here, and if you think you're protecting Angelique by squirrelling her away, think again.

The press know you're here, they know you've had medical specialists in. The stories about you and Angelique are getting wilder.'

'Have I poisoned him yet?' asked Angelique.

'No, you've had a riding fall and are at death's door. That or you're undergoing artificial insemination with my brother's teenage sperm—that you kept *frozen for years* in a facility meant for horse sperm—'

'Ew...'

'I hear you.' Valentine threw up his hands. 'I'll prepare a statement and have the palace announce it tomorrow.' He glanced her way, his expression shuttered. 'I could announce our engagement and upcoming wedding at the same time as well.'

'I haven't said yes.'

And there it was. Happy-clappy noises on the surface and a deep unease about stepping fully into his world underneath.

'You're stuck with me either way, you realise.'

'But he would, of course, prefer his heirs *legitimate*,' Vala emphasised, with a glare for them both.

'I'm working on it,' he replied coolly. 'Butt out, Vala. And, Angelique, brace yourself.'

'I'm ready.' She summoned a smile.

'Liar.'

Hard to deny. 'Are you willing to deny paternity?'

'Never.' His eyes flashed dark warning. 'You know this.'

'Then I'm ready.'

* * *

The news did not go down a treat. It was one thing to make the foreign horsemaster with the terrible reputation and sultry good looks his mistress. It was quite another to inform a nation they had twins on the way.

Angelique said very little beyond, 'Told you.'

If it bothered her more than that, she didn't let it show. Her family closed ranks. No comment from any of them or any of their employees. Not one leak from the house of Cordova and that in itself was impressive. No lovers coming forward to spill the beans. Angelique had responded to that with a funny little smile and words that held the sting of hidden truth. 'I've only ever had one lover, so if you want to give an interview, go ahead. The rest of my reputation is pure fabrication—some of it planted by me for reasons I thought valid at the time. For protection, even. It protects me still, in that if I'm never given a chance to succeed, I can never try to win the hearts of your people and fail.'

'That's your approach?'

'What's yours?' she enquired politely, far too politely for it to be anything but a warning. 'Ram me down people's necks until they swallow?'

Yes. Faint heart would get him nowhere. 'Yes! We run positive press to counter the negative. We stand united. I go on record more often to express my joy at the thought of starting a family with you. We get married. Do you know how many articles here are calling me out for not offering to marry you? Dozens! What good a king who rules by example not being prepared to stand up and protect his family? And don't even start with the "we're not good together" line, because I won't believe you. I'm yours. You're mine. Across time. You know it's true. Why won't you even consider it?'

It was the closest he'd ever come to begging.

'Can't you see I'm a liability?' she countered. 'It will take years, a lifetime, before I am fully accepted by the good people of Thallasia. Maybe on my death bed, at which point I will hopefully be unable to raise my middle finger in response to such largess, but I will be thinking it and you will know it and laugh and kiss me and tell me your life has been richer than you ever imagined it could be. That you never regretted loving me—not for one minute. That you're proud of our children who are wonderful people. That you'll think of me every day with joy. *That's* what I will consider a life well lived. Not what your papers think of me today or tomorrow or after the birth of two more souls for your royal machinery to shape. Who wants to inflict a life of service onto their children? Not me!'

'It's not all *bad*, Angelique. Yes, there are constraints, but we can still be royal and raise children who are wonderful people. It's not all tyranny and tiaras and nothing else. You could do such good. *As my wife.* Why won't you let others see you the way I do?'

'Hear! Hear!' said a male voice from the doorway, and there stood Theo with Moriana next to him. 'Is this a bad time to call?'

'Kings,' muttered Angelique, but then turned and curtseyed and hardly blushed at all. Nothing like airing dirty laundry. Valentine suspected his colour was a dull red too.

Moriana smiled brightly and flowed into the room, a vision of modern elegance, and Valentine could clock the difference between her and Angelique, of course he could, and he'd still choose Angelique's heart and passion and fire every time. Didn't she *know* what she brought to his table?

'Theo thought we might, oh, I don't know, go cavorting with you both in public. Somewhere with horses or children or fluffy kittens.' Moriana glanced at her husband. 'To show our support for you both, no matter what kind of union you choose.'

'She also mentioned piles and piles of leftover paella,' added Theo. 'It's the only reason I'm here. Valentine didn't call for reinforcements against the future mother of his children who has misguided thoughts of ignoring her public image. At all. We didn't drop everything to get here.'

'Well, thank God for that,' muttered Valentine and strode forward to clasp hands with Theo and embrace Moriana. 'Otherwise I'd owe you both a favour, and that never ends well.'

'You mean never ends well for you,' murmured Moriana. 'I vote we all ride the grounds of this estate and then return for a private dinner between friends that may or may not involve leftover paella made by Angelique's mother.'

'But Angelique's pregnant. With twins.'

Moriana looked at Valentine blankly. 'I know. Everyone knows. Bravo.'

'He thinks I shouldn't ride,' Angelique supplied helpfully.

'Oh, for—' Whatever Moriana had been going to say was cut off by her husband's elbow to her ribs. 'Ow.'

'A drive, then,' said Theo. 'Very civilised. Or a buggy ride. I love a good buggy ride.'

The man was very clearly mad, but a buggy was duly found and royal horses trucked in from the palace. A photographer arrived too, and the following day a series of happy photographs appeared online to help sway public opinion. Wedding or not, King Valentine of Thallasia had welcomed the Cordova woman into his inner circle.

Angelique read the half a dozen news articles about her that now turned up on the kitchen table every day, courtesy of the father of her unborn children. In truth, it had been no hardship, sitting in the open carriage and listening to tales from the daily horse-back processions that had proceeded Moriana's wedding to Theo. The ridiculous pageantry they'd endured in the lead-up to their wedding. A cavalcade of horses, the black steeds of Arun against Liesendaach's greys. The village welcomes, the charities they'd arranged to visit every single day. The medieval-style tournaments at the end of each day that had brought spectators by the thousands and money into every place they'd stayed. Angelique had never laughed so hard as she had at Moriana doing her 'Ice Queen with ants in her pants while sitting astride a horse at the end of a long day and she simply had to pee' impersonation, but there was no peeing yet because she still had to listen to an earnest city mayor announce her by every title she held, and then welcome her to their very beautiful city, and *then* list the name of every last person who'd helped them prepare for her.

'But you did get to pee, eventually,' Theo had drawled.

And when Moriana had replied, 'Like a horse,' that had been the end of Angelique's composure.

Their visit seemed to relax Valentine, and for the next few days he backed off, just a little, when it came to treating Angelique like a priceless porcelain doll.

Pregnant, yes. Slow to start some mornings. But she was real, and warm and they were in this together.

And during those nights when he held her close and passion got the better of them, she thought that maybe, just maybe, she could be what he needed.

CHAPTER ELEVEN

'YES,' SHE SAID, one evening a few days later when they were back in his palace and getting ready for bed. 'I want a small wedding, and by that I mean tiny, with only your family, my family, and one or two others present, and I want to have it in the little tiny chapel here, the one with the stained-glass window that catches the setting of the sun, but yes. I'll marry you.'

The look on his face.

The lovemaking that followed.

No matter what the world served up as punishment for daring to think she could be enough.

She'd never forget.

Confusion ruled Valentine in the time leading up to the wedding. It turned out that sex was an excellent antidote to actually addressing the issues likely to plague them once Angelique became his Queen. The limitations she would have to accept. The knowledge she'd have to absorb if she wanted to represent the crown and do so without fault. He could protect her from the worst of it, he knew he could. But first she had to listen to him and at the very least acknowledge that, in regard to all things royal, his experience would serve her well.

She knew the news articles about her—and him—were brutal, but had told him she didn't read them. She missed horse-riding but never mentioned it in front of him. His head of security informed him that she'd taken up jogging through the woodlands as part of her daily exercise routine.

Their wedding banns went out, and instead of a formal picture his publicity team had shown one of Angelique teaching Juliana how to ride and sharing a smile, while he looked on from a few steps away. They'd chosen it because Juliana's delight and Angelique's pride in the young girl's achievement had made him look happy and approachable. A man rather than a king, and a novel approach for his publicity team to take, but it seemed to be working.

Sometimes.

On occasion.

In between the more vitriolic pieces in the press.

Protocol lessons began for Angelique, and folders full of rules now sat on her work desk alongside breeding logs and bloodline registers.

'It's okay,' she would say to him. 'I've got this.'

Moriana and his sister tossed the rule books aside in favour of offering Angelique practical lessons in palace etiquette. They took her under their wings, only to have her emerge hours later, pale faced and subdued, with eyes lit from within by worry rather than happiness.

'Nothing to it,' she'd deadpan, only her hand would be shaking when he enfolded it in his, and she'd sag against him as if hoping for strength, and then he'd go berserk with wondering if she'd been on her feet too long and end up sweeping her into his arms and depositing her on the nearest soft surface while he buried his face in her neck and simply breathed her in.

He could give her everything but her freedom.

'Let's go riding,' he said the following morning as they lay in a tangle of rumpled sheets and sunbeams, and she edged up onto her elbows, her dark hair a messy cloud and her expression still warm and open—not yet shutting down beneath the demands of the day.

'Did you not ban me from horse riding? With the full approval of my traitorous parents?'

He had. Not one of his more logical decisions. 'I was thinking you could borrow Juliana's pony and I could ride a quiet horse to match and we could go to the hunting lodge for the day. Just like old times.'

Absolutely nothing like old times, her arched eyebrow told him.

'I'll throw in an open fire and a catered meal when we get there,' he added.

'I'll take it,' she said. 'With one condition.'

'Name it.'

'I need help with the list of charities your sister left for me to look at. I'm supposed to pick half a dozen and become their patron. And, sure, I can put a tick beside half a dozen of them in ten seconds flat, but what will it *mean*?'

Which was how two days later they ended up in a sitting room stuffed with velvet furniture, velvet drapes and heavy carved wood tables, throwing goose-down pillows in a circle in front of a dancing fire and asking for hot coffee, tea and chocolate for three, as his niece and Angelique spread out on their stomachs on the pillows and looked to him and the dozen or so files full of paperwork for answers.

'Should you be lying on your stomach?' he asked Angelique, because, what about the babies?

'It's very comfortable at this point in time, Your Majesty,' she replied with a wink towards his niece. 'Would you care to join us?'

Surrender seemed inevitable. He sank onto a cushion, legs crossed in front of him, unbuttoned his blazer rearranged his cuffs and straightened his tie. 'Presentation matters,' he began. 'It makes others feel that you're making an effort for them. It's a way of showing that you value them and those things they stand for. Will you value me?'

Juliana sat up immediately. Angelique followed. 'Who *are* you?' she murmured. 'Do I know you?'

'As His Majesty the King? No, I don't believe you do. But just as I discovered another you when in the presence of your family, it's time for you to see another side of me. Who am I, Juliana?'

'King Valentine II, by the Grace of God, King of Thallasia, Defender of the Faith,' the young girl answered immediately.

'And what do I do?'

'You govern Thallasia according to the laws and customs of the land. You offer law, justice and mercy in all your judgments, in the name of God.'

'And?' he prompted, while Angelique looked on.

'And you do so willingly, with a glad heart, a sound mind, and a spirit of...' The little girl faltered.

'Service,' he offered quietly. 'We live to serve.' Heavy concepts for a seven-year-old. Parroting the words back at him was only the start of coming to terms with what they meant. 'And there are very few circumstances where we can decide not to do that and just walk away.' He held Angelique's gaze. 'Even if we fall madly in love with someone and want to do whatever makes them happy, we still can't walk away from our duty. That's why only very special people choose to marry us, and even when we rejoice that they *want* to marry us we worry we'll break them, because it's hard to serve this country day after day, year after year, decade after decade, and sometimes the criticisms outweigh the thankyous. And when that happens and people start saying bad things about us, what do we do?'

'Cry?' said Juliana. 'Because that's okay, but not

in front of people. Only some people, like you or Mama or nanny Chloe.'

'Maybe,' he murmured. 'Maybe we do cry in front of our special people, but then we wash our faces and see if what the people are saying is true and we really can do better next time. And the time after that and the time after that until we're doing a much better job a lot of the time and people don't say nearly as many bad things about us any more. But sometimes that takes years.'

'I have years,' Angelique promised quietly, and in that moment his heart truly did break for her, because he loved this woman so much, and he really had put her in an untenable position.

'They're crucifying you.'

'I have you,' she said next, and he wanted to cry on his own behalf now, because he wasn't enough, he would never be enough to counter all the freedoms she would lose. 'You're right here, telling me about the things that drive and inspire you, and I have our babies in my belly, and members of your family to get to know and I will learn how to do what you do, and it won't always be enough but it will always be my best. This I promise you.'

He cleared his throat of its sudden tightness and reached for the first folder. 'I'll read them out and you can say yes, no or maybe. Juliana, this goes for you too. And then we can examine those options you like in depth. Number one. Libraries and literacy for children?'

'Me!' said Juliana, and he nodded and placed the folder in front of her.

'And why might Angelique not want that one also?'

'Because she's a grown-up?'

'Because she can barely read Thallasian?' Angelique offered. 'Maybe adult literacy is my jam.'

Valentine nodded his approval. 'Next. Mobility for the disabled. Including therapy horses and the roles they play in rehabilitation?'

Juliana's hand was up in the air and she looked fit to burst.

Angelique raised her hand too. 'Could we both become patrons of this one? Because I have some ideas and I'd like to know more. Horses or not.'

He created a middle pile. 'Heart Foundation? Rare Cancer Awareness? Alzheimer's research? The medical ones are always hard to choose from because the need to shine a light on their research goals is always there. But what we can do is make connections. We raised funds for the national college of music by tasking them with performing in small groups for Alzheimer patients and filming those concerts. Charitable donations went up thirty per cent for both causes that year. Performing throughout the elderly community became a permanent outreach programme for the orchestra. Some of the young musicians we showcased *still* visit those nursing homes to play for old friends, and once a year, Juliana, your mother invites the musicians and carers and doctors and researchers to a big luncheon in the blue ballroom. That's just one of the things you can do when you decide to lend the might of your royal name to a cause. And the trick, if it's a trick, is to make people feel good about helping others, and to say "I see what you did there" and "thank you". It can be about connecting people who can help each other. It's not always about raising money.'

'What's your hardest patronage portfolio? The one you work hardest at but never seem to get anywhere?' asked Angelique, and he didn't have to think twice for an answer.

'Domestic violence.' Darkness lived there. He'd barely scraped the surface with his own father. It could have been worse. It *was* worse for so many people.

'Then I want that one too,' Angelique said. 'I've never lived it, but I want to share that load with you. Will you let me?'

'I'll have it sent to you.'

She shouldn't smile at him as if he'd given her the world.

'Would you like to run away with me to your hunting lodge and get married tomorrow?' she asked. 'It would solve a lot of internal debate about empire waistlines versus regency ones.'

'Sorry. We need the spectacle.'

She sighed. 'What *are* your thoughts on empire waists versus regency ones?'

'They're very convoluted thoughts.' He had no idea what she was even talking about.

'Do you have a tiara?' the little Princess wanted to know.

'No. But I do have a mantilla,' Angelique replied. 'It's a lace veil that's been in my family for many years, and it has a special comb that goes with it that makes it sit up just so.'

'There are tiaras available for—' he began.

'No.' It was a very cool no, even if accompanied by a softening smile. 'I will not deny my heritage and I will not disappoint. You just need to trust me on this.' She gave Juliana a wink. 'I am on the look-out for the perfect pair of earrings, though. Diamonds.'

They both turned to look at him, and he obliged with a theatrical sigh. 'I suspect I can help you there. What about a necklace?'

Angelique shook her head. 'No need. The neckline of the dress I'm partial to is too high.'

'Bracelet?'

'The sleeves are too low.'

'Is there any skin on show?'

'Not a lot, no. It's a gown of many buttons. Very demure. And don't say, "You? Demure?" because that would be the wrong reply altogether.'

He did have some tact. 'Doesn't matter how modest the gown, it's you I'll be looking at.'

She searched his eyes as if looking for the truth in his words. 'Are you sure?'

Because you don't have to go through with this,
her own eyes seemed to say.

Every so often she touched on this with him as
if to gauge whether the publicity had grown savage
enough or her ignorance of royal protocols was prob-
lematic enough that he might wake up one morning
and think no.

She was a mad mix of 'I've got this' coupled with
'I know this isn't what you signed on for'.

Surely her insecurities would fade once they were
married? Or maybe her baby-making hormones were
holding her hostage to doubt and it would take longer.

Until then he'd simply have to be sure for her.
'I'm sure.'

They were doing okay on the 'we're getting married in a few days' time' front. Valentine, for all
his fiery emotions when first hearing he was to be
a father, and the mad protectiveness in the weeks
thereafter, had managed to find some kind of balance that allowed him to be supportive without being
overbearing. Loving without being smothering. Encouraging without being condescending. He seemed
happy with his lot, with *her*, and his confidence in
her ability to be the Queen Consort he needed her
to be never wavered.

No pressure.

She tried not to let the pressure get to her, but
the closer she got to her wedding day, the more An-

gelique knew something had to give. She couldn't keep learning how to be a royal wife, and a royal patron, and give Juliana riding lessons, and run her own stable from afar, and be a mother to twins once they arrived.

She had to let go of her old life in order to fully embrace this new one.

'I'm heading to Spain on Friday to tie up some business commitments,' she told Valentine when he arrived at the manor after spending yet another evening at a charity banquet without her. He attended so many, and he did not complain, but sometimes when shedding his uniform or dinner suit he seemed to shed his strength along with it, nothing left in the tank for her but a smile and silence until they hit the sheets and he lost himself in her warmth.

He worked harder than anyone she knew—including her father. He had very little downtime now that he was fully back at work. Trying to have an everyday conversation with him often felt like loading him up unnecessarily. And yet she wasn't one to hold back when it came to sharing the parts of her life that he wasn't involved with.

He lay stretched out on her bed, still half dressed, with half his face buried in a pillow, his one visible eye closed, dark lashes fanning across his perfect features, and he might not have been looking at her but his ears still worked and his groan said a lot.

'No.' One word, muffled but unmistakable, and

then he rolled onto his back, his eyes mere slits as he regarded her with a frown. 'I can't get away.'

'You don't have to get away. I'll go alone. I'm only going home.'

'No.' He put the heels of his hands to his eyes as if he had a headache brewing.

'If it's a security issue, I'm sure I'll be—'

'Fine? No. There'll be no leaving the country without me. Bring your work here.'

'But the horses and the people are there.'

'I *said* no. You'll stay in Thallasia until the babies are born, and after that there will *still* be no leaving the country without me.' He levied himself to a sitting position on one edge of the majestic bed. 'That's just the way it is.'

'But…what do you think is going to happen?'

He didn't answer her.

'Do you think I won't return?' He wouldn't look at her. 'Valentine?'

'It's about risk management, nothing more.' He still wouldn't look at her.

'Because I will return, if that's what you're worried about.' They were getting married in less than a week.

'It's not.'

'I've given you no cause to doubt me.'

This earned her a sullen stare. 'Like I said, it's a risk-analysis decision, not an emotional one. I've commitments here and cannot accompany you, therefore you cannot go. Sorry.' He didn't sound sorry. He sounded resolute. 'Surely you realise this is how it goes?'

'I realise this is how you want it to go,' she offered mildly. 'But engaged, married, or soon-to-be parents—we're still individuals. I don't expect to accompany you every time you pop over the border for a business meeting. Do you expect me to?'

'No.'

'Didn't think so.' They stared at each other in stony silence.

'Humour me,' he said finally.

'You don't think I'm going to return.' How could he possibly think that?

His silence was telling.

'You're having second thoughts,' she said next.

'No.' He was quick with his answer. 'No. But you might be, now that you know what marriage to me is going to take.'

'I signed your piece of paper. I gave you my word. I'm not leaving you.'

He said nothing. Still waters, this man. And very deep, very turbulent emotions. An image of his underground river flashed before her. He would cope with her absence, of that she had no doubt, but he would do so with the coping mechanisms available to him.

'Okay, let's make a deal. I stay here for you, you do something for me.'

His eyes narrowed even further. 'I trust you to know how far you can push me.'

Big of him. 'I want permission for my family to visit here or at the palace any time they or I choose.' She needed them in her life. Always had, always would. 'If I can't get to them, they need to be able to come to me. They're my strength and I'm going to need them.'

'Done.'

'And I want Carlos, Benedict, Luciana and your sister to be godparents to our children.'

'Absolutely not.' He reared up onto his elbows. 'Three of them are terrors. I'd say all four were unsuitable, but I don't know your brother well enough to tell.'

Snort. Her brother was the most centred of the lot, this was true. 'You don't think our children will be high spirited and in need of guidance from those who know exactly what they'll likely get up to? These are *our* children we're talking about.'

'Point. I'll consider it.'

But she was already shaking her head. 'Not good enough. The power in our relationship can't rest wholly with you. I will bend on the matter of not returning to Spain. I'll give you the peace of mind you seem to need. And in return you'll do the same for me.'

He could push the matter if he wanted to. Refuse her request and limit her freedom. Keep the upper hand and be every bit the man his father had been when it came to personal relationships and authoritarian rule.

But in the end, he chose differently.

'Done,' he murmured. He might have preferred to choose differently, more strategically, and cut her family out of selection. But unconditional love and a sense of belonging mattered too, and, from what he'd experienced, the people she'd chosen would provide it. 'I accept your choice of godparents.'

Her brilliant smile made him shake his head and smile.

He'd wanted a woman who would challenge and impassion him, he reminded himself silently. One who had no hesitation when it came to calling out his insecurities and insisting on fair treatment. He could do this—learn to accommodate her as they went through life together. Learn to trust her opinions and instincts and be ready to bend if they disagreed. He wanted his people to value her as he did, and if that meant leading the way, then lead he would.

'You'll need to take my best security detail with you, and I'll still worry from the moment you leave until the moment you're back in my arms, but if your business in Spain is that important that you need to be there, you can go.'

He had an armful of Angelique moments later, her eyes shining with tears as she let loose a string of impassioned Spanish, and he had no idea what she was saying—but it was likely something along the lines of 'You wonderful, complicated, fascinating, treasure of a man. I love you.'

She kissed him hard and fast, and then again, and that second time felt like a thank you. 'You fool!'

Oh. So… Not even close.

'I love you,' she said next, and that was more like it. It was the first time she'd said it. He would hear more of it. Embrace it. Commit to a lifetime of loving her too.

'My future Queen and mother of my child, I'm all in. No matter what it takes, I love you too.'

CHAPTER TWELVE

ANGELIQUE DIDN'T GO to Spain—she brought the horses and buyers to her. World-class polo players were an odd lot, but tell them she was selling her first and second string polo ponies—twelve altogether, preferably to be sold in two groups of six—and she was stunned by how many of them were willing to travel to see her.

Her father, who usually conducted sale negotiations, would always be on the other end of the phone for her and they knew it. But the horses were hers—selected and brought on by her, not to sell, that hadn't been what she'd meant to do with them at all, but with children on the horizon and queenly duties to contend with, and Valentine to make time for, something had to give. She'd always been a trainer first and a rider second. Those invitations to try out for World Championship events had been gratifying but not the end game where Cordova ponies and reputations were concerned.

She'd even fielded an enquiry from the newly minted billionaire who couldn't ride.

He'd been taking riding lessons, he said.

He'd offered her an apology for his behaviour, no excuses. His sister had threatened to disown him if he didn't stop treating people like they were mud on the bottom of his overpriced shoes, he'd said. Having money had not made him a better person, he'd confessed. And even if she had no desire to sell him any Cordova ponies, or to accept his apology, he was indebted to her for speaking out as she did when no one else around him would.

It made her think. It made her examine her own hot-headed responses and realise that she needed other ways to make her point if she was to stand at Valentine's side and do good.

She'd always been altogether willing to call out poor horsemanship, but maybe there was another way of pushing for change that didn't involve arguing with insecure billionaire shipping magnates in public. Give the man riding lessons. She almost choked on the thought, but what if she'd encouraged him to improve rather than humiliating the man?

She penned a reply before she could overthink it. The horses were in all likelihood already sold to professional players, but he was welcome to visit the Cordova estate in Spain. She was offering a tour of the facilities there, either her father or their head groom would see to that, and insight into how Cordova ponies were trained. She'd been placed on the back of a horse before she could walk. Becoming a skilled practitioner in any sport took time and if he really had caught the polo bug she knew good people who could help him on his way.

Her old self scoffed, figuring he was playing her and all he wanted was to buy her horses.

Her new self thought life journeys took so many twists and turns that giving a person the benefit of the doubt might just be a good thing.

'I have to become a better person than I am,' she told Valentine later that evening.

'For the babies?' he asked, and she hadn't even *thought* of that angle.

'Yes. For the babies, and for you and for all the people who are going to have to rely on me now to know how things work and do the right thing and not lose my temper at the slightest provocation. Oh, this is bad. I'm two minutes into the mere thought of self-improvement and already I'm failing!'

Valentine set a steaming cup of green tea in front of her, and she liked green tea, but wanted to weep at the thought of limiting her caffeine intake for months on end.

'Hormones have a lot to answer for,' he murmured. 'No one is saying you have to be perfect. No one ever is.'

She wrapped her hands around the warm cup. 'You're kind of perfect.'

'It's official. Baby brain is real. You've lost your mind.'

'I'm scared.'

'I know.'

'I don't want to let anyone down.'

'I know that too.'

'We get married on Sunday.'

'Yes.' He gathered her in, ran his hands over her body. 'Do you need me to distract you?'

'Yes.' Please God, yes, before she drowned beneath the weight of a foreign crown and her ever growing insecurities. 'I want you to do your very best.'

She found a buyer for her top six horses in an old friend from Argentina. His name was Enrique, horses were his life, and he was currently the number two ranked polo player in the world. He'd tumbled Carlos ten years or so ago now, before Benedict, and he and her brother had not remained friends afterwards. He'd always been civil to Angelique and Luciana though—even at the height of their notoriety. She had a soft spot for him and he had the money to buy and the weight of his international polo club behind him. Her horses would thrive in his care and shine on the field. He was the perfect match for her beloved ponies, no question.

He was married now with two young children and a partner he loved to distraction. His phone was full of pictures of his ranch and family. Benedict—her brother's partner—was a brilliant, complex prince of a man, and she liked him for her brother very much, but this man could have been her brother-in-law had the world turned a little differently, and she wouldn't have been disappointed.

She was practically selling her horses to family.

This was what she told herself as she shook hands on a deal that would put more money in her pocket than she'd ever earned before, and then she had to go and spoil her professional persona by choking on hot tears. He saw her struggle, he was standing right in front of her, and wrapped her in his arms in an instant. He was a confident, compassionate married man giving comfort without thought.

It didn't look that way the following morning with a full colour picture of her and Enrique embracing and a headline to go with it that made a mockery of the truth, of her values, and of Valentine, King of Thallasia.

The Real Father Revealed!

A headline for the ages, and the words beneath it weren't much better. Never mind Enrique's loving family. Never mind her upcoming wedding at the weekend. She was the worst kind of soulless schemer and Valentine was the worst kind of fool. She tried to set the paper aside and get on with her day, but Valentine had been staying at the palace these past two days on account of a water management convention being held in the capital that he'd attended, and she hadn't been able to get hold of him this morning.

He'd *know* it was a lie, wouldn't he? Berate her for letting another man hug her in public, maybe, and for feeding the negative-publicity machine, but it hadn't been deliberate. The photo had to have been taken by one of the grooms or the security staff. An opportunist looking to make a quick killing, nothing more. Or maybe she should read significantly more into it—a last-ditch attempt by palace courtiers to derail her marriage to their King. The thought made her want to throw up, or maybe morning sickness was the reason. Nothing she could do to stop her twenty-minute visit to the bathroom.

She was sitting on the restroom tiles, her back against the wall and a porcelain toilet bowl her closest companion, when her phone rang in the other room and she almost let it ring out but it might be Valentine, so she got to her feet and made a dash for it, hoping her stomach wouldn't choose this moment to revolt. Nothing left in it anyway.

It wasn't Valentine. It was Carlos. She could picture him reading the same paper she'd just read, Benedict seated opposite, both of them baffled by her naiveté. They'd taught her better than this.

She hadn't expected her brother's anger, but it spat down the phone line. 'What on *earth* do you think you're doing?' he asked icily, and she closed her eyes and took herself back to the bathroom and sat back down against the wall.

'This is about the article in the paper?'

'Enrique? Seriously? I know you've always had time for him, but what the hell was he doing anywhere near you? Why? Why would you let yourself be photographed with him like that just days before your wedding to a king who's fighting for the right to be with you with every breath he takes?'

'I know. I know. I didn't mean to, it was just a mistake.' She took a deep breath and hoped he would understand. 'I sold my horses. All of them.' Eyes closed, with her head in her hand, the phone to her ear and her voice small. 'I figured I needed to commit to being Queen Consort completely, so I sold all my horses to a brilliant polo player and an honourable man, and then I cried like a baby at the loss of an identity I've worked my whole life for.'

Silence greeted her words, and then Carlos swore, and she cut the call and threw the phone across the floor. It came to rest on white tile, the screen now shattered, just one more visual reminder of how thoroughly unsuitable she was to be anyone's queen. Too fiery and emotional. Too stupid to keep her head down and not bring shame upon the people who loved her.

So many rules, and she didn't know them all and might never know them all and it mattered now more than ever because she wasn't just representing herself any more. She *knew* that.

Valentine would have every right to be furious with her.

Carlos was. The brother she'd driven her tattered reputation into the ground for hadn't even thought enough of her to listen when faced with a picture of her in his old lover's arms.

She spent forty more minutes in the bathroom, alternating bouts of tearful self-pity with the dry heaves of morning sickness. Her stomach settled eventually, and she stripped off to take her second shower of the morning and start the day afresh. She couldn't face heading down to the stables today and the work would be all but finished anyway. She'd say goodbye to her horses tomorrow night when everyone had left for the day so there'd be no one around to witness her tears.

But if not jodhpurs, what would she wear? She stared into the closet full of demure new clothes carefully selected with her new role in mind and couldn't even choose one that wouldn't make her feel like a fraud. In the end she reached out and randomly plucked a dusky pink dress from the hanger—its feminine colour muted by simple lines, a modest crossover neckline, a fitted waist and a flared skirt that ended just below her knees.

She plaited her hair and rolled it into a bun and added the moonstone and white gold earrings her parents had given her for her twenty-first birthday and a matching bracelet that had come from Luciana. A pendant necklace from Carlos completed the set and she put that on too, with shaking hands. He had to be looking at that photo with different eyes now, surely? He had to know how much the sale of her horses had cost her. He'd come round.

She tried not to dwell on how badly his criticism had shaken her. The rest of the world could go hang, but her people, the ones who knew her inside out, when they acted up she trembled.

As for what Valentine might think...

She reached for the engagement ring he insisted she wear whenever they were in public. A priceless diamond from the bowels of the royal vaults, to be sure. An enormous glittering bauble and a total pain to wear and maybe once she was married and had a perfectly plain wedding ring to wear, she could set it aside and only wear it on special occasions.

If she got married.

The news article she refused to glance at again had truly done a number on her. Gold-digger, schemer, conscienceless liar, foreign filth. The King's Downfall.

Maybe she wouldn't be getting married after all.

Valentine knew something was afoot when his head of palace affairs swept into his quarters at a quarter past seven with Vala hot on his heels. Neither looked pleased to be there.

'Problems?' he asked. 'Because I'm due at the conference at nine to introduce the British delegation.' He'd planned to spend most of the day there— hopefully soaking up information like a sponge. One swift glance at the newspaper on the tray his secretary held out towards him made a mockery of that plan.

The headline was hard enough to swallow, but the accompanying picture landed like a blow to his heart. Angelique enfolded in the arms of another man, clinging to him as if he was her everything. 'Who is he?'

'A polo player,' his sister said.

He recognised the background. They were on the grounds of the duchy Angelique rented from him. She'd brought another man inside the manor. 'When was he there?'

'Yesterday.'

'And who took the photo?'

His secretary grimaced. 'One of our security personnel. They've been relieved of their post, Your Majesty.'

Betrayed by someone whose job it had been to protect him and Angelique. It had happened to him before and would happen again. Never got any easier to bear. 'Good. Cancel my conference duties and tell my driver I'm going to see Angelique this morning.'

'Your Majesty, shall I alert Ms Cordova as to your imminent arrival?'

'No.'

'I can accompany you,' his sister began.

'No.'

'But—'

'I'm not angry.' He spoke true. 'I'm disappointed by the gross invasion of privacy, but it happens. Peo-

ple get greedy. As for the insinuation that I'm not
the one who is the father, those rumours have been
circulating since the beginning.' He waved his hand
towards the paper. 'Take it away. There's nothing
new to see.' Except Angelique's spectacularly bad
judgment and choice of friends to snuggle into, a
little voice inside his head suggested helpfully. And
the jealousy threatening to cloud his eyesight with
a blood-red haze if he had to look at the picture for
one more second.

His secretary beat a hasty retreat. His sister
stayed, her gaze concerned. 'Do I have to remind
you that our father's temper was not his best feature?' she asked, and that itself was warning enough.

'Do you see me frothing at the mouth?'

'No, but I see the look in your eyes. Are you sure
you wouldn't rather cool down before you speak
with Angelique?'

Go take yet another dip in surging, freezing cold
water in an attempt to get a handle on his emotions?
He wasn't angry. Not in the hot-headed way that
usually assailed him. This anger was cold and pa-
tient and aimed directly at those who would destroy
the best thing that had ever happened to him. 'No.'

'Should I come with you?'

'To see my beloved?' That earned him a hard
glare. 'No.'

'Just don't say anything you're going to regret.'

'You mean like ask why she placed herself in such
a compromising position in the first place?' He mir-

rored his sister's dark glare right back at her. 'She doesn't know life beneath the microscope yet. As you say…she'll learn.'

Angelique was sitting at her dressing table of her small side bedroom when he arrived, and he stood in the doorway a moment and watched as she played with the engagement ring he'd given her weeks ago. She looked as beautiful as he'd ever seen her, all soft femininity and flawless features. Beautiful and unutterably sad at the sight of his ring.

Any small sliver of anger at the thought of her hugging the polo player evaporated, replaced by concern for her well-being. If she'd seen this morning's paper she already knew what her unscripted hug had cost them.

He watched as her gaze found his in the mirror, full of misery and wordless apology.

Guess she had seen it.

'Put it on,' he said, and she shook her head as if she would deny him.

He softened his voice and vowed to keep his cool. 'Put it on and tell me what happened, and if I can fix it, I will.'

'You can't fix it. You'd have to fix me.' Her eyes filled with tears. 'I didn't mean to get so upset that Enrique felt he had to comfort me.' She still hadn't put the ring on. 'He's a good player. With them, he'll be the best. They couldn't have gone to a better home.'

'What are you talking about?'

'I sold my polo ponies.'

He didn't understand.

'Didn't make sense to keep them.' Her smile wobbled. 'I'm pregnant. I'm going to be something else from now on. What use did I have for them? I just didn't think it'd be so hard. I was there when every one of them were born. I delivered half of them, nurtured them. All my father's knowledge and mine went into selecting them to keep. They were my companions and my confidants. My identity. Mine. All gone. Paid for in cash by the highest suitable bidder.'

Her sacrifice threatened to split him open with the force of his feelings. She'd given up everything for him, to be with him, even her beloved horses, and his people had repaid her with slander and rejection. 'You didn't have to sell them.'

'Yes, I did.' She put the ring on and took a deep breath and turned to stand and face him, beautiful and elegant in all her fine clothes. He barely recognised her, she was so tightly composed. He'd done this to her. Stripped her of everything she held dear. 'Aren't you supposed to be somewhere else this morning?'

'No.' He took her in his arms and felt her sag against him. Such a slight woman for all her wiry strength. 'You didn't have to. We'll get them back for you, and you can—'

'I can what? Compete? Stay a horsemaster? You know I can't.'

'You can if I abdicate.' He meant it. 'Marry on Sunday, put Vala on the throne on Monday and walk away. Say the word and I'll do it. I love you. Quite desperately. You have to know that.'

She buried her face in his neck and clung. 'I thought the article would send you into a temper.'

'It did, but not in the way you're thinking. Thallasia doesn't deserve you and nor do I, but I plan to spend the rest of my life convincing you I do.'

'You're not angry with me about the photo?'

'I'm extremely angry about the photo.' He would not lie. 'But not with you. And seeing as I'm about to try and buy your horses back from your handsome polo player I'd best not turn on him either.'

She pulled back to look him in the eye. 'They're not going to stop writing terrible articles about me.'

'Not for a while, no. But, Angelique, I know they're rubbish. I know your heart, and it's mine, and whether I deserve you or not I'm not letting you go. So pick a road and watch me walk it with you.'

He couldn't stand it when she cried, and she cried long and hard, another waterfall to drench the front of his snow-white shirt. Maybe there was something wrong with him, but he far preferred their emotions out than in. This bedroom—their private places— were not for stoicism or secrets. They were for loving and being loved and letting feelings flow.

Finally, she stepped away and wiped at her eyes

and looked at her fingers and hiccoughed a laugh. 'They always say the mascara is waterproof and it never is.'

The streaks on his shirt seemed to prove her theory correct, as she turned back to the mirror and reached for a tissue and wiped the make-up away. She picked up a mascara tube as if to start all over again, and then met his gaze in the mirror. 'You really love me enough to walk away from your duty?'

'It's breaking you. And, yes.' If that was what it took to make her whole again, then yes.

She ran her finger over the engagement ring and shook her head as if to object. He'd never seen anything more beautiful than a tear-drenched Angelique Cordova reaching for her inner strength.

'I'm not broken.' Her mouth firmed. 'I'm hormonally challenged because I'm pregnant and I'm coming to terms with a new way forward. That's all it is. And you don't need to relinquish your crown in order to prop me up. Not now. Not ever. I'll learn, we'll learn, together, and maybe one day we'll laugh about our mistakes, because you know what?' She flung the words at him like a challenge.

'Tell me.' He played the part she offered him with a keen sense of anticipation.

'I'm going to be the best Queen Consort your country has ever had.'

CHAPTER THIRTEEN

THE KING OF THALLASIA's wedding day bloomed warm and bright, with a blue sky overhead and the scent of roses, sweet peas, and the faintest hint of jasmine of the night wafting through the air. The press reports were encouraging. There was nothing like a royal wedding to make a nation hope for the best. The modest chapel located deep inside Valentine's palace walls had been dressed with flowers from the heartlands of Thallasia and the far mountain regions of Spain, and framed the entrance to the place of prayer with splashes of green, soft whites and creams, and deepest crimson.

Valentine fidgeted, and his sister tutted and swiped at his hand to stop him fussing with his cufflinks once again. Vala had taken on the role of groomsman, because if a king was going to break tradition and marry in private why not go all out and have a woman to attend him?

He wanted no other to stand with him, no matter her gender. She was his twin.

The chapel only had room for a dozen or so guests—the seating consisted of one long pew on either side of a central aisle, repeated so as to be only three rows deep. Where to sit three kings, their queens, assorted children, and the immediate family members of the bride had been a problem, but Vala had sorted it, and that result too eschewed tradition. Vala's husband, daughter and twins in the first pew closest to him. Angelique's mother with King Theodosius on the other side, with room for Angelique's father once he delivered her to the altar. Moriana in the pew behind them, glowing with late pregnancy, with Benedict and Carlos alongside her. Queen Consorts Ana of Byzenmaach and Sera of Arun sat across the aisle from them, with Ana's little girl nearest the aisle for the better view. A couple of kings stood sentry at the rear, one on either side of the door, ready to open it as soon as directed to. Give them something to do other than stand there and look pretty, Vala had said, and she'd got away with it too. Luciana, in her role of bridal attendant, would slip in beside whichever king she chose, after making sure Angelique's bridal veil and train were just so and following along behind her sister and father on the way to the altar. A simple wedding.

A beautiful day for it.

Prayer candles sat in wall sconces carved from stone a thousand years ago. A single stained-glass window with the picture of a sun in the sky and a castle and verdant farmlands beneath it took the full force of the late afternoon sun, sending scattered light patterns across the walls.

Private. Intimate. Perfect.

So perfectly right, his decision to take this woman as his bride. To serve at his side. To brighten his day and warm his nights. To love beyond measure for as long as he drew breath.

And every last person in the room knew without doubt that his vow to do just that would hold.

He'd loved this woman since they were both eighteen years old, and this time he would love, honour and cherish her.

There was no music to announce the arrival of the bride. The music would come later, when they had their first dance as man and wife and then everyone gathered around a perfectly informal round table for a wedding feast prepared by the mother of the bride. The most glorious cooking smells had assaulted his senses every time he'd drifted past the kitchen that morning.

The fact that the wedding feast table had been dressed with a king's ransom in bejewelled and golden tableware only added to the feeling that this blending of cultures and ancestry and families was something truly special.

He'd been pacing the halls all day, waiting for the morning, and then lunch, and then the afternoon to pass so he could get to the getting married part of the day and beyond.

Whoever had decided a sunset marriage would

be just the thing for him to bear clearly had a master's degree in psychological warfare.

Vala and Moriana had suggested the time, if memory served correct.

Figured.

But that time was upon them now, and, at the faintest of knocks, Cas and Augustus reached for the chapel doors and pulled them open, and there stood Angelique, bathed by the light of the setting sun filtered through precious stained glass.

He wasn't the only one to gasp and hold his breath.

He might have been the only one to hold his breath until Angelique took her first step forward.

And then more steps, until her father handed her over and stepped back, and then it was only the two of them and the archbishop and repeating words and vows that described all the love he had to give. To have, to hold, to honour, serve and protect. To love, deeply and wisely, and he knew, when he finally raised the veil to reveal his wife, and the sun shone down on them and bathed them in a golden glow, that his choice had been the right one and that he had permission from above to love as he would.

The kiss, when it came, was as reverent as he could make it, what with the aching need to sweep Angelique into his arms and carry her off, into that sunset, on a pair of horses bound for the hunting lodge, but he resisted.

That was for later. Her horse had been decked

out with a flower harness. His stallion was the fastest one in his stables, Alessandro had assured him.

Guess they'd find out later if that was true or not.

He resisted the urge to sweep her away as they ventured hand in hand down the aisle and braved a rainfall of rose petals flung at them by kings who did silly, spontaneous things in private that they'd never do in public.

Resisted through the first dance in a near empty ballroom before someone bribed the string group to play heavy metal.

Resisted through the lone photographer's plea for fifteen minutes of their time, and the resulting selection of half a dozen photographs to release to the press that evening.

Relaxed through the dinner, and, by the time the speeches came, he tossed the one he'd laboured over and simply spoke from the heart.

'To my family and friends who have stuck by me all these years and lent their support to my choices…

'To my wife's family, my thanks for gracing me with one of their own…

'To the people outside these walls who are counting on me to rule wisely, with compassion and love, and in the name of duty to the crown… I will not let them down.

'And to my wife, whose love, and grace, and tolerance make me a better man. Angelique, there are some new horses in the stables. Enrique helped me choose them and so did your father and Alessandro.

They tell me they show promise. Their bloodlines are magnificent. They will delight and challenge you, so I'm told. Never feel guilty about spending time with them. Nurture them, take joy in them, because I want you to have passions that will sustain you. Besides me.' Ad libbing had its flaws, the sniggers that followed reminded him so. The arrogance of kings, tamed, and bent towards love. 'They are my gift to you because, although together we will endure, I will not allow the weight of the crown to swallow who you are. A toast.' He raised his glass. 'To my wife. Horsemaster Cordova.'

Not a traditional toast by any stretch, but necessary, here and now amongst this lot, so many of them who knew what it was like to lose track of themselves in service to crown and country.

There were more toasts.

And dancing. Dear heaven, the ridiculous dancing. Who needed a million-dollar DJ and a warehouse full of smoke machines and chemical stimulation when you had this lot?

Benedict had ordered a disco ball and it turned out they had one. They put *Pulp Fiction* to shame, and no one died but bribery material was collected for the ages.

The photographer had been banished hours earlier and the children had all been tucked up in bed. Which begged the thought, 'Are you by any chance ready for bed?'

His glowing bride bestowed on him a wicked

smile that promised heaven, and said, 'I've practised wedding goodbyes for three days solid. I've memorised titles, compliments, invitations for people to join us that I know won't clash with their calendars. Moriana helped.'

'Of course, she did.' That woman was a menace to royalty everywhere.

'I reckon I've got it down to three minutes solid if no one interrupts.'

'Hey, everyone!' He held his hand high. 'Thank you for coming. We need three minutes of your time and then we're gone.'

Angelique had never spoken so fast. She'd forgotten about all the hugs people insisted on giving her, but they were out of the room in five minutes.

Angelique had never been so happy.

Valentine, on the other hand, was tugging her in the wrong direction. 'Where are we going?'

'The hunting lodge.'

'Now?' She was all for surprises but there was a perfectly good turret and a king's bedroom two storeys up in the other direction. It had candles and chocolates and champagne and white bedding in it. A vase stood ready for her wedding bouquet and her bridal nightgown had been set out in all its glory in his dressing room. She'd arranged everything.

'The hunting lodge is all set up for our wedding night.' His grin promised a good one. 'Palace staff have been there all afternoon getting it ready. There are no stuffed monkeys anywhere in it, I promise.'

His staff had clearly been very, very busy, what with getting two places ready. They really had to work on co-ordinating their surprises.

She walked with him through the palace doors and nearest gardens. Two horses stood waiting at the edge of the herb garden, one of them with what looked like a whole carrot plant in its mouth and a garland made of flowers around her neck.

She knew that horse as she knew her own re-flection.

It was her favourite mare. The one Valentine had ridden so successfully a few months back. The first of her first string of polo ponies that she'd sold to Enrique. The other horse was big and black, a stallion, Thallasian bred, no question.

'She's yours again, with Enrique's blessing,' he whispered in her ear. 'But is she faster than my fastest stallion? That's the question.'

This gorgeous, generous man in front of her was hers, and she was his.

And the journey beckoned.

EPILOGUE

HE WAS NEVER having sex again. The fact that he'd
said this aloud in a birthing room filled with far too
many people…okay, four other people…meaning
Angelique, Luciana, a midwife and a royal physi-
cian, as well as him, served only to show him how
truly panicked he was. Because King Valentine of
Thallasia was a cool, calm and considered monarch,
not prone to blurting out the first thought to enter
his head. Even if he was currently sitting behind
Angelique, on a birthing bed, so as to provide a bul-
wark for her to lean on and hands for her to crush
every time the midwife said push.

'I swear—'

'No swearing in front of the babies,' Angelique's
twin said cheerfully, although he noted a certain
tenseness around Lucia's eyes that suggested she
wasn't exactly unaffected by the longest labour in
the world either. 'What do you think, Angelique?
Do you intend to hold him to the no-sex-ever-again
plan?'

Angelique looked up at him, long strands of silky black hair sticking to her neck and forehead. Escapees from the plait she'd pulled her hair back into several decades ago.

It sure as hell felt like several decades ago.

'I mean, it could be the only thing he has going for him,' Luciana added, wicked to the end, but if it made Angelique smile—which it did—he would forgive her twin the overreach.

'No sniping,' Angelique told them.

'But it keeps me sane.' Luciana strode to the business end of things, took one look, paled, and walked briskly back to her sister's side.

'I agree. It's our thing. The bedrock on which we base our friendship,' he added. Anything to avoid thinking about what might be happening, or not happening, and he just wanted someone to *do* something to ease Angelique's pain. 'Take the sniping away and we'll be mute.' He played his part, silently scanning Luciana's face for reassurance she couldn't give.

He had no idea what was happening other than his wife was in pain and had been for an eternity.

'Okay, mama,' the midwife said from way down where he was never going again. 'This is the one. Imagine the rolling waves pushing the little seashell further up the sandy beach each time. Gentle rolling waves, and if a big fat wave comes along, don't fight it, go with it, because it's going to push that little seashell right to your feet.'

Possibly not the best time to remind the woman

that this was a landlocked country or mention that the river running beneath the castle was a ferocious, tumultuous beast with a history of being used for punishment. Besides, Angelique's homeland had azure beaches, gentle waves and sunshine, so who was he to deny her the pretty imagery? Whatever worked, right? Because something had to work for her soon. They'd been at this for over twelve hours already.

He couldn't take much more.

'Deep breath,' said the midwife suddenly, and there was an air of command in her voice that had never been there before. 'Hold it… And push hard, *now*!'

Angelique pushed, her teeth clenched and her eyes tightly closed, as if directing all her energy southward. Too tense, the midwife had told her when they were only a couple of hours in. Still tense, he thought, and trying to stay in control.

'I'll roar if you will,' he whispered. 'I'll start.' Who cared if the first noise his children heard was their father screaming for them to come out and face his wrath for giving their mother such a hard birthing time?

He was a protective man. Very.

They'd find out soon enough.

Luciana met his gaze and he wondered if he looked as terrified as she did. She nodded, and rallied around his challenge. 'I'd like to see that.'

He pressed his lips against Angelique's temple for

a moment, tightened his hold, flung his head back and roared. Full volume, holding nothing back. Not the pain nor the joy of living and loving as he would, not the agony of seeing the woman he loved in pain. Suffering, for him.

Luciana joined in.

'You're both mad.' But Angelique pushed and joined her voice with theirs and twenty seconds later his daughter was born.

'Well, that's one way of doing it,' offered the midwife dryly as she handed the baby to the doctor and went back for seconds.

Not three minutes after that, his son arrived in the world, his voice almost as loud as the rest of his family's. Someone placed his daughter on Angelique's chest, skin to skin, and it was an image he would carry with him for ever. There were tears. Some of them might have been his.

Then the midwife was ordering him to stand up and take his shirt off, and Angelique lay smiling, and Luciana started laughing like a loon before leaning over to kiss her sister's cheek before stepping away. 'I'm out of here to tell the family the good news.' They were all out there—every last Cordova, and Benedict too, and Valentine's sister and her family and probably the ghosts of all the rulers of Thallasia. 'A future queen for Thallasia. How about that?'

How about that, as the midwife showed him how to hold his son and cradle him to his chest.

'Don't drop them,' said Luciana, and then she was gone.

'I'm going to kill her,' Valentine announced, now terrified of dropping his baby. 'Are they healthy, the babies?' And hot on the heels of that thought, he turned to Angelique. 'Are you okay? Is my wife okay?'

Angelique's 'I'm okay' got lost beneath the midwife's answer that she was doing very well.

He couldn't stop looking at the two tiny miracles in their arms. 'They're so beautiful.' He should have expected as much, given the gene combinations involved. God knew, he and his sister had been feted for their looks from the moment they were born, and still were. As for Angelique, some would say her looks had been her downfall. 'How do we make them plainer?'

'We don't.' His birth-battle-hardened wife smirked at him. 'We all have our burdens to bear. Take me, for example: I have a husband who's never having sex again.'

About that... 'I could be persuaded to revisit that particular edict.'

'You do that.'

'I love you, you know.' The words came from deep down inside. 'You're everything I've always wanted. You. Them.' He nodded towards the babies. 'Us. I'm never letting this go.'

Smiling eyes regarded him fondly. 'Good thing I'm in it for the long haul, then.'

A fact for which he was eternally grateful. 'Together, then.' So many blessings had been bestowed upon him. 'Let's go rule the world.'

* * * * *

If you fell in love with
Pregnant in the King's Palace
*why not catch up on the previous instalments in
Kelly Hunter's Claimed by a King miniseries?*

Shock Heir for the Crown Prince
Convenient Bride for the King
Untouched Queen by Royal Command

Available now

WE HOPE YOU ENJOYED
THIS BOOK FROM

HARLEQUIN

PRESENTS

Escape to exotic locations where passion knows no bounds.

Welcome to the glamorous lives of royals and billionaires, where passion knows no bounds. Be swept into a world of luxury, wealth and exotic locations.

8 NEW BOOKS AVAILABLE EVERY MONTH!

#3921 NINE MONTHS TO CLAIM HER
Rebels, Brothers, Billionaires
by Natalie Anderson

CEO Leo revels in his stolen moments with an alluring mystery waitress. Only later, when their paths collide in the boardroom, does Leo discover she's reluctant socialite Rosanna. And carrying his twins!

#3922 THE INNOCENT CARRYING HIS LEGACY
by Jackie Ashenden

Children? Not for illegitimate Sheikh Nazir Al Rasul, whose desert fortress is less intimidating than his barricaded heart. Until surrogate Ivy Dean appears on his royal doorstep...and he finds out that she's pregnant with his heir!

#3923 SECRETS OF CINDERELLA'S AWAKENING
by Sharon Kendrick

Cynical Leonidas knows he should keep his distance from innocent Marnie, yet discovering his Cinderella needs urgent financial help prompts an alternative solution. One with mutual benefits, including exploring her unleashed passion even as it threatens to incinerate his barriers...

#3924 THE GREEK'S HIDDEN VOWS
by Maya Blake

To gain his inheritance, divorce lawyer Christos secretly wed his unflappable assistant, Alexis. Now it's time to travel to Greece and honor their vows...publicly! Yet as they act like the perfect married couple, their concealed chemistry becomes overwhelming...

#3925 THE BILLION-DOLLAR BRIDE HUNT
by Melanie Milburne

Matteo has an unusual request for matchmaker Emmaline: he needs a wife who *isn't* looking for love! But the heat burning between them at his Italian villa makes him wonder if *she's* the bride he wants.

#3926 ONE WILD NIGHT WITH HER ENEMY
Hot Summer Nights with a Billionaire
by Heidi Rice

Executive assistant Cassie has orders to spy on tech tycoon Luke. While he's ultra-arrogant, he's also aggravatingly irresistible. Before Cassie knows it, they're jetting off to his private island—and her first-ever night of passion!

#3927 MY FORBIDDEN ROYAL FLING
by Clare Connelly

As crown princess, I must protect my country...*especially* from infuriatingly sexy tycoons like Santiago del Almodovár! He wants to build his disreputable casino on my land. And I want to deny our dangerous attraction!

#3928 INVITATION FROM THE VENETIAN BILLIONAIRE
Lost Sons of Argentina
by Lucy King

To persuade the formidable Rico Rossi to reunite with his long-lost brother, PR expert Carla Blake must accept his invitation to Venice. She knows not to let powerful men get too close, but can she ignore their all-consuming attraction?

YOU CAN FIND MORE INFORMATION ON UPCOMING HARLEQUIN TITLES, FREE EXCERPTS AND MORE AT HARLEQUIN.COM.

HPCNMRB0621

Get 4 FREE REWARDS!

We'll send you 2 FREE Books plus 2 FREE Mystery Gifts.

PRESENTS

His Majesty's Forbidden Temptation

NEW YORK TIMES BESTSELLING AUTHOR
MAISEY YATES

PRESENTS

What the Greek's Wife Needs

USA TODAY BESTSELLING AUTHOR
DANI COLLINS

Harlequin Presents books feature the glamorous lives of royals and billionaires in a world of exotic locations, where passion knows no bounds.

FREE Value Over $20

YES! Please send me 2 FREE Harlequin Presents novels and my 2 FREE gifts (gifts are worth about $10 retail). After receiving them, if I don't wish to receive any more books, I can return the shipping statement marked "cancel." If I don't cancel, I will receive 6 brand-new novels every month and be billed just $4.55 each for the regular-print edition or $5.80 each for the larger-print edition in the U.S., or $5.49 each for the regular-print edition or $5.99 each for the larger-print edition in Canada. That's a savings of at least 11% off the cover price! It's quite a bargain! Shipping and handling is just 50¢ per book in the U.S. and $1.25 per book in Canada.* I understand that accepting the 2 free books and gifts places me under no obligation to buy anything. I can always return a shipment and cancel at any time. The free books and gifts are mine to keep no matter what I decide.

Choose one: ☐ **Harlequin Presents Regular-Print**
(106/306 HDN GNWY)

☐ **Harlequin Presents Larger-Print**
(176/376 HDN GNWY)

Name (please print)

Address   Apt. #

City   State/Province   Zip/Postal Code

Email: Please check this box ☐ if you would like to receive newsletters and promotional emails from Harlequin Enterprises ULC and its affiliates. You can unsubscribe anytime.

Mail to the Harlequin Reader Service:
IN U.S.A.: P.O. Box 1341, Buffalo, NY 14240-8531
IN CANADA: P.O. Box 603, Fort Erie, Ontario L2A 5X3

Want to try 2 free books from another series? Call 1-800-873-8635 or visit www.ReaderService.com.

*Terms and prices subject to change without notice. Prices do not include sales taxes, which will be charged (if applicable) based on your state or country of residence. Canadian residents will be charged applicable taxes. Offer not valid in Quebec. This offer is limited to one order per household. Books received may not be as shown. Not valid for current subscribers to Harlequin Presents books. All orders subject to approval. Credit or debit balances in a customer's account(s) may be offset by any other outstanding balance owed by or to the customer. Please allow 4 to 6 weeks for delivery. Offer available while quantities last.

Your Privacy—Your information is being collected by Harlequin Enterprises ULC, operating as Harlequin Reader Service. For a complete summary of the information we collect, how we use this information and to whom it is disclosed, please visit our privacy notice located at corporate.harlequin.com/privacy-notice. From time to time we may also exchange your personal information with reputable third parties. If you wish to opt out of this sharing of your personal information, please visit readerservice.com/consumerschoice or call 1-800-873-8635. **Notice to California Residents**—Under California law, you have specific rights to control and access your data. For more information on these rights and how to exercise them, visit corporate.harlequin.com/california-privacy.

HP21R

SPECIAL EXCERPT FROM

H HARLEQUIN

PRESENTS

Cynical Leonidas knows he should keep his distance from innocent Marnie, yet discovering his Cinderella needs urgent financial help prompts an alternative solution. One with mutual benefits, including exploring her unleashed passion even as it threatens to incinerate his barriers…

Read on for a sneak preview of Sharon Kendrick's next story for Harlequin Presents, Secrets of Cinderella's Awakening.

Almost as if he'd read her mind, Leon caught hold of her and turned her around, his hands on either side of her waist. She held her breath because his touch felt *electric*, and he studied her upturned face for what felt like a long time before lowering his head to kiss her.

It was…dynamite.

It was…life-changing.

Marnie swayed in disbelief, her limbs growing instantly boneless. How was it possible for a kiss to feel this *good*? How could *anything* feel this good? At first there was barely any contact between them— just the intoxicating graze of his mouth over hers.

He deepened the kiss and began to stroke one of her breasts. Her nipple was pushing against her baggy T-shirt dress toward the enticing circling of his thumb. Was it that that made her writhe her hips against his with instinctive hunger, causing him to utter something in Greek that sounded almost *despairing*?

The sound broke the spell and she drew back—though in the faint light, all she could see was the hectic glitter of his eyes. "What… what did you just say?"

"I said that you set my blood on fire, *agape mou*. And that I want you very much. But you already know that."

Well, she knew he wanted her, yes. She wasn't actually sure about the blood-on-fire bit because nobody had ever said anything like that to her before. And although she liked it, her instinct was not to believe him, because even if it were true, she knew compliments always came with a price.

Yet what was the *point* of all this if she was just going to pepper the experience with her usual doubts and spoil it? Couldn't she have a holiday from her normal self and shake off all the worries that had been weighing her down for so long? Couldn't she be a different Marnie tonight—one who was seeking nothing but uncomplicated pleasure? She had always been the responsible one. The one who looked out for other people—with one eye on the distance, preparing for the shadows that inevitably hovered there. Wasn't it time to articulate what *she* wanted for a change?

She cleared her throat. "Would you mind speaking in English so I can understand what you're saying?"

She could hear the amusement that deepened his voice.

"Are we planning to do a lot of talking, then, Marnie? Is that what turns you on?"

Something warned her she'd be straying into dangerous territory if she told him she didn't know what turned her on because she'd never given herself the chance to find out. But while she didn't want to lie to him, that didn't mean she couldn't tell a different kind of truth.

"*You* turn me on," she said boldly, and something about the breathless rush of her words made his powerful body tense.

"Oh, do I?" he questioned, tilting her chin with his fingers so that their darkened gazes clashed. "So what are we going to do about that, I wonder."

Don't miss
Secrets of Cinderella's Awakening,
available July 2021 wherever
Harlequin Presents books and ebooks are sold.

Harlequin.com